Richard Hooker Wilmer, George P. C. Rumbough

From Dust to Ashes

A Romance of the Confederacy

Richard Hooker Wilmer, George P. C. Rumbough

From Dust to Ashes
A Romance of the Confederacy

ISBN/EAN: 9783337348298

Printed in Europe, USA, Canada, Australia, Japan

Cover: Foto ©Andreas Hilbeck / pixelio.de

More available books at **www.hansebooks.com**

From

Dust to Ashes.

A Romance of the Confederacy.

MOST RESPECTFULLY DEDICATED

TO THE GALLANT DEAD OF THE ALUMNI OF
THE V. M. I.,

WHO KEPT THEIR FAITH

AND

LAID DOWN THEIR LIVES AS SOLDIERS OF THEIR MOTHER
STATE, IN THE CONFEDERATE WAR OF 1861–65.

ALSO,

TO THOSE WHO FELL IN THEIR CHARGE ON THE
MEMORABLE PLAIN OF NEW MARKET,

THE "BOY SOLDIERS;"

BEARDLESS YET DAUNTLESS;

TO THEM WE BEND IN FAITHFUL ACKNOWLEDGMENT OF
SERVICE, AS GLORIOUS AND UNDYING, AS THOSE
WHO CLASPED THE SHEEPSKIN, THE SINGLE
TOKEN OF THEIR ALMA MATER.

Dedication.

We are growing old, and soon the "taps" will be sounded for the last of the classes preceding 1861. 'Tis only a desire to render our homage unto truth, the great Director of Happiness in this world, that we humbly, most humbly present this truthful statement to those who may perchance find these lines. Names may be changed, but behind every line, truth stands ready to prove every assertion, and prepared to repel every charge of wrong.

May a just God, remembering the woes of the conquered, and the pride of the oppressor, give us and our children a heart to bear our cross, and a memory whereon shall be engraved the eloquent language of Doctor Cave—

"I am not one of those who, clinging to the old superstition that the will of heaven is revealed in the immediate results of trial by combat, fancying that right must always be on the side of might, and speak of Appomattox as the judgment of God.

"I do not forget that a Suwaroff triumphed and a Kosciusko fell; that a Nero wielded a scepter of empire and a Paul was beheaded; that a Herod was crowned and a Christ crucified; and instead of accepting the defeat of the South as a divine verdict against her, I regard it as but another instance of 'truth on the scaffold and wrong on the throne.'"

LITTLE ROCK, ARKANSAS, 1895.

Respectfully,

THE AUTHOR.

VIRGINIA MILITARY INSTITUTE.

PREFACE.

READING one day, the "explano-prefatory" of a book entitled, "In Vinculis," by A. M. Keiley, a Virginia Confederate, I saw these words: Through books, newspapers, magazines, military commissions, congressional legislation, proclamations, reports, "novels," so-called, and histories that are far more romantic, the North is not only writing the story of the late war, but the character of its late enemies. A great deal of this, from proclamation up, we know to be false, but the time has not come, nor does every one who feels the need, feel the power to do justice.

Each Southern man though, may, and ought to contribute something to our own story of this war, even though it be as pure a trifle as this: "The living claim it, and the inexpressibly loved and honored dead demand it."

And I hope to live to see the day, when the infamous atrocities of Hunter in the Valley of Virginia will have a fitting historian.

And above all, when the story of that hellish carnival of lust, and rapine, and outrage, and arson, and murder and nameless villianies which Yankee poets and magazine writers euphoniously name, "The great march from the mountains to the sea," shall be painted with a broad brush and a free hand, that mankind may shudder again to think of the crimes committed in the name of "Liberty."

Actuated by just such feelings and motives, I thrust out into the world, this new born "trifle," to bear all the ills of a doubting and critical world.

There is not an event of any magnitude mentioned herein, that is not critically and historically true. It is needless to say that naught is put down here in malice; the days of carnage are long past, and no spirit of retribution exists in the breasts of the unsuccessful, but there is a

spirit implanted in the minds of all true and honorable
men, to know the truth of events, whether detailed in history or in romance. In no instance, throughout these
pages, is an effort made to exaggerate the deeds of our
enemies, or to insult the dead by false representation; as
an instance, the deeds of Miss F., absolutely perpetrated
during and after the war, if left to our judgment alone,
were far more heinous than those detailed herein.

> Ah! me, the forty years since last we met,
> Seems to me forty folios, bound and set
> By time, the Great Transcriber, on his shelves,
> Wherein are written the histories of ourselves.
> What tragedies, what comedies are there;
> What joy and grief, what rapture and despair!
> What chronicles of triumph and defeat,
> Of struggle, and temptation, and retreat;
> What records of regrets and doubts and fears!
> What pages blotted, blistered by our tears;
> What lovely landscapes on the margin shine;
> What sweet angelic faces, what divine,
> And holy images of love and trust,
> Undimmed by age, unsoiled by damp or dust.
> —LONGFELLOW. (*Morituri Salutamus*).

FROM DUST TO ASHES.

A ROMANCE OF THE CONFEDERACY

BY GEO. P. C. RUMBOUGH.

LITTLE ROCK, ARKANSAS.
Published by the Brown Printing Company.

FROM DUST TO ASHES.

CHAPTER I.

IT was the 4th day of July, 185—, when the Corps
of Cadets of the Virginia Military Institute at
Lexington stood for the last time, with the graduating class of that date, on the parade ground,
and, while the last sad, sweet notes of "Auld
Lang Syne" floated upon the air from the in-
struments of Volandt's Band, with tears and
almost a heart-broken voice came the Commandant's order, "Break ranks." Then came from
a lusty, cheery voice, "Three cheers for 'Little
Gill!' "(the commandant). This was given with
energy and zest, and for the day discipline was
discounted.

To one among those cadets, who wore a captain's chevrons, how ominously sounded those
words, "Break ranks!" For years the barracks
of the Institute had been his home; now his
ranks were broken by command, his home was
broken. To break ranks was to drift far away
from the blue, outlined mountains; from the ties
of devoted room-mates, not changed for years;
and, from her who had won the adoration of his

heart. All, all seemed to be gliding away, as did the fading tones of that sad "Auld Lang Syne."

Amid the chaff and chattering of elevated plebean corporals, more modest, but not less exalted sergeants, lieutenants and captains, whose happiness was tempered with dignity, four roommates, including our captain, sauntered quietly to their double-tower rooms, to lay aside sword, sash and gun; to shake off forever the dust of college, and prepare to step forth a citizen, to do duty in the great struggle of life, liberty and pursuit of happiness.

Upon the evening of this day, the great event of the four seasons, the annual ball of the graduating class was to occur, under the auspices of our captain, whose taste and energy had given the walls and ceiling of the Mess Hall the appearance of a thousand lights, reflecting the colors of every nationality, and dazzling the eyes of the beauties of many states; but, none more charming than those of the daughters of the grand old Commonwealth of Virginia.

It is now the hour of midnight, and three cadets, Capt. Phil Randolph, Lawrence Mayne and Robert McKene are engaged in close conversation, apart from others. Speaking in a nonchalant way, Capt. Randolph remarked, "I suppose you two will report progress after the ball?"

With downcast eyes, poor Lawrence answered,

THE BALL.

sadly, that he feared that he would have nothing to report "worth mentioning," for be it remembered, though as true and honest a man or a soldier as any living being, he is not of the mould, nor gifted with nature's happy faculties, to impress or captivate the feminine heart. Imagine a young man about twenty-one years of age, five feet and eleven inches in height, body flat and angular, a waist too near his shoulders, and which always enforced an unseemly crease in his uniform coat near the hips. His ears were large, his nose long and thin, and a mouth too broad for his face, and eyes neither blue, black nor gray, but verging toward hazel, they were cheerful and expressive; his hair was thin and straight—too straight. With this faint outline you have our dolorous friend, Lawrence Mayne.

The brother room-mate, Robt. McKene, was just the reverse—perfect in figure, stout, strong and active. His head was crowned with wavy brown hair, and set with sparkling, laughing gray eyes. In a cheery, happy manner, which always characterized the man, he said: "Steady, Lawrence, a fig for a faint heart in the beginning of the action; remember old Jack's talk at our last recitation: 'Remember, gentlemen, when it becomes necessary and war is declared, and the sword is drawn, throw away the scabbard.'"

"Don't mind that handsome upstart. I don't

like his bearing, or his hypocritical familiarity; that Mr. Van Horton, I mean."

"Oh, Rob, you are always my guardian angel."

"*Je suis ce que je suis,*" remarks Lawrence, "and for better and for worse. I can't hold a candle to that blarsted fellow; and moreover, she, to whom he now talks so earnestly, is from the same State up north, and there is where the additional advantage comes in."

Three ladies are now approaching, each leaning upon the arm of her escort, for the merry dance has been in full swing for three hours, and while the musicians are being refreshed, the couples are promenading to see and be seen.

"Come," was the one word spoken by Captain Randolph, and with smiles and happy greetings each swung in upon the unoccupied side of his respective lady-love. The old adage of a new broom applies here, and not many steps are taken before the three room-mates are left each in the sweet possession of the object of his affection. We will not weary the reader with a lengthy description of these young ladies, but simply say that Captain Randolph was bending his head low and speaking to a typical southern beauty, clear complexion, cheeks tinged with the rich, roseate hue of the peach-bloom, shaded by hair as dark and glossy as the raven's wing, and eyes lustrous, beautiful (ravishing) black eyes, with a pliant and petite figure; as such we introduce Miss Marguerite Darlington.

With Robert McKene was the tall, lithe blonde, the pretty and talented first born of a neighboring pastor, in whose love he felt secure, each bound not only by affection's tie, but by a similarity of faith, being both communicants of the same denomination, and as was often said around the table when books grew tiresome, that "they were born for one another."

With Lawrence Mayne came the vivacious little blonde from New York, Miss Sadie Carday, whose petite form was enhanced by contrast with her partner. Her head was thrown back, crowned with innumerable yellow curls, her piquante face upturned and her blue eyes reflecting those of enraptured Lawrence, smiling and nodding with that same sweet little "yes," "yes," "really," which we had heard so often in our hours of leisure, when rules were broken and visits stolen. As we look back now, a feeling of sad and weary recollection pervades our whole being.

The events of that night of music, the dance, the merry voices of the revellers, are the memories of happy hours, the glimpses of bright sails, cloudless skies, a smooth and unruffled sea; no sign of storm, of hidden reef nor mountain billows; no shipwreck, no deeds of bloodshed, no thought of grim-visaged war or of sudden death.

The evening is spent, the lights are extinguished, and each room-mate is happy in the escort of his lady-love home.

The 5th of July finds the coaches all busy in loading cadets and baggage for a homeward journey, and our heroes depart, swearing allegiance unalterable and undying; and thus the dust of college is shaken from their garments, and left behind forever.

. . . .

Four years later, a tall, soldierly-looking man is leaning carelessly against a stanchion of the guards of one of the floating palaces of the great Mississippi river; his gaze is fixed upon the seemingly moving landscape, as the big boat ploughs its way through the muddy waters. It is growing towards the close of the day, and a stillness pervades the hour, only broken by the escape of steam and the splash of the wheels. Clad in a hunter's garb, with high-topped boots, one would hardly recognize the beau, Captain Randolph, or him who was one time called the best dressed man in the western city of M——.

It grows late, but still he keeps his place; there is a step near him and he incidentally turns and meets the gaze of a stranger, bearded like himself. Approaching, he asks, in an insinuating voice:

"Is this not Captain Randolph, who was so attentive to the beautiful Marguerite Darlington at the ball in Lexington a few years ago?"

The answer comes slowly and deliberately:

"I believe it is, sir; but, pardon me, who are you?"

"Well, I took the advantage of your roommate, and now I have done the same for you. Well! well, my beard is my protector, as the lapse of four years has given me this advantage—but, in truth, I am the Van Horton, whom Miss Sadie Carday introduced to yourself and friends. I am glad to meet you, as I am now hurrying north from New Orleans. The Crescent City is a little too warm for my comfort, thermally and politically, and I long for home and a more congenial condition of politics; but there goes the gong; let us sup, and over our cigars this evening talk of old times and of those to come."

Seated in the saloon, Van Horton meets the calm and earnest gaze of Randolph, and abruptly asks:

"What do you think of this firing on Fort Sumter?"

With a coolness born of a spirit of contempt, engendered four years before, Randolph answers: "That they meant business, and burnt some powder."

Quickly questions Van Horton:

"Oh! but I mean what about the South, and will Virginia go out?"

"The South," answers Randolph. "I fear means war. Virginia will be the last to go out, but afterwards, like her Washington, will be first in the war."

With the air of one indulging in a speculative soliloquy, Van Horton adds:

"It looks strange, Randolph; here we are, two good friends; we have no quarrel; we have supped at the same table, danced in the same quadrille, and now we are to make ready to cut each other's throats; and for what?"

"There you are too hard for me," answers Rando'ph. "I claim the right of secession, and the principle of States' Rights, but the *policy* of secession I utterly condemn as the quintessence of folly. As you Northerners first in everything weigh the almighty dollar, if you want a cheap trade, in the cause of humanity, it would take an incubus from the shoulders of the Southern slaveholders, and cost millions less in dollars, and thousands of precious lives, to follow old England's example, purchase the slave and colonize him in his native land."

Stung by the answer, Van Horton retorts, testily:

"But your people have degraded the flag of our country, and replaced it with another; in fact, are inaugurating a rebellion, are personally rebels."

"Now, stop there," said Randolph, rising up briskly. "You misrepresent, either from ignorance or from prejudice, and I will not hear it; we own no parent government, as Washington did Great Britain, nor do we call it rebellion to differ with our brother; and for the future—"

But here the loud voice of the steamer's whistle, which effectually drowned all efforts at being heard, checked all conversation, and caused our disputants to join their fellow-passengers forward of the cabin, where the view of the bluffs of Fort Pickering and Memphis, crowned with its long line of brick houses of business, the tall spires of its houses of worship and its long blank walls of ample cotton sheds greeted the eyes already grown tired of the sameness of river scenery, of sand-bar, snags, sawyers, cotton fields and fringing willows.

With many bumps, and a river song by the crew, whose refrain, "Jee rang! oh, ho!" was given in chorus with a will, and not without melody, the stage plank is lowered, and the passengers are now leaving who have Memphis for their destination. Slowly going up the bluff, Van Horton stopped, looked back and greeted Randolph with the words, "Gayoso, I suppose, Captain?"

"Yes, answered Randolph, I always stop there; the proprietor, Cockrell and his boys are old friends of mine."

"I shall go there too, remarked Van Horton, if only to stay long enough to tell you where I am going, and say good-bye."

Oppressed with the companionship of an uncongenial acquaintance, Randolph rather sneeringly answered:

"Perhaps the thermometer which stood so high in New Orleans may read a few degrees higher here, and what is said, had better be delivered in transitu."

And as they walked only a few blocks distance, Randolph learned that Sadie is the affianced of Van Horton; that she has discarded Laurence Mayne, who even now has been one of the foremost to enlist in the Confederate cause, and in her eagerness to vent her patriotic zeal, has written to her fiance Van Horton to come back to his native state and enlist in the ranks of its defenders; and winning glory, to be rewarded with smiles and affections of his devoted Sadie.

"Passengers going north by the Memphis & Ohio—all aboard!" cries the porter.

"Good-bye, Randolph, we may meet again; who knows, and where?"

And the form of Van Horton disappeared, and Randolph observed nothing, for his back is turned to the rattle of the 'bus.

CHAPTER II.

IT is a bright, sunny morning, when the young day is still lingering to kiss the dews of night; the stillness of nature is only broken by the cock-crow from the lovely valley resting so peacefully under the shadow of the mountain spurs which now interpose their heads to the rising sun, waiting for the day-god's higher ascent to reveal its sylvan charms, and happy homes. Near the highway stood a plain but well-kept cottage; the summer roses had not all fallen, and the well-kept vines which clung to the porch, lattice and tree, with potted plants of fuschia, heliotrope and other hot-house growth scattered here and there, showed the presence of refinement and gentle woman's taste.

D A—2

An old man sat upon the porch, in gown and slippers; a man of eighty years, with bald head, but above the neck, fringed with hair as white as snow; his beard was long and like that of his head was snow white; he was seated in a large rocker, quietly reading his Bible; his good wife, a woman of some seventy years of age, as straight as an arrow, with jet black hair and features lovely in her old age, with hazel eyes which beamed love in every glance, stood near.

The family servant, the only one left after their fallen fortunes and emigration from Virginia, and a member of the family for forty years, with bucket in hand, stood at the front gate, on her way to the spring; but, hearing horse-hoofs up the road, she stopped and stood gazing, until a stranger, clad in gray, with his old blue slouched hat pulled over his eyes, and mounted upon a horse which looked able to dare and do what his master's rein and spur directed, drew up alongside of the gate, and with a gently-spoken "Whoa!" looked into the old, familiar face and said:

"Mammy, is this the way you welcome your baby?"

The bucket dropped; Randolph was hauled from his steed, and with such expressions as "My God! that I shouldn't know my child!" was hugged and kissed and thumped in the back

MAMMY'S SURPRISE.

by his good old black mammy, until rescued by
his mother and father, who, in their quiet way,
by gentle effort, came to the rescue, and welcomed their boy with smiles and kisses and
loving words.

With the appearance of the youngest child, a
girl of sweet sixteen, a bright and happy mortal,
with the figure of a goddess and a face to match,
lovely lips and laughing, blue eyes and bonnie,
brown hair—the pet sister of our hero, the clamor
of tongues, inquiring, admiring and wondering,
would have upset and silenced a man of even
sterner stuff than our hero.

"Well, Master Phil, honey! you did fool me
that time sure," says mammy, and off she goes
into one of those stereotyped laughs, that was
as dear to his ears, as it had lingered always in
memory.

The good, old hands fondled his hand and
smoothed his hair, and, having caught her
breath, continues:

"And, honey, where have you been? What
have you been doing? So tall and straight, with
the same kinky head of my baby boy!"

And while all this is going on the sister is kissing the cheeks and lips of the soldier brother,
while the aged parents are sitting helplessly
smiling and drinking in the comforting joy
begotten by the unexpected and happy return

of their boy to their hearts and home. But, ah! how soon was that joy to be changed to sadness, by an absence shrouded in the smoke of battle and poisoned by the raids of ruthless robbers.

"My son," says the father, "I see that you have on our color, but where is your command and what is your rank?"

Randolph answers that he is captain on staff duty, but now on special service to Columbia, South Carolina.

"But, tell me, father, how do you like the mountains of Tennessee?"

"You understand, my son," answers the old man, "that this is East Tennessee, and there are many ignorant mountaineers, who are not patterns of nobility in any sense, and they claim to be good Confederates, when our troops hold the country, and are equally positive that they are good Federals when the Yankees are here; they are robbers at heart, and I expect to contribute to their rapacity, but not without an effort of my old arms to protect my own; but tell us of the news; we are twelve miles from the railroad, and news by letters or papers seldom reaches us."

Randolph then proceeds to tell of the battles around Fredericksburg; of the second Manassas, of Sharpsburg, the raging and gallant defense of Fort Sumter, and of Battery Wagner, and the

sinking of the Keokuk, much of which he was
an eye-witness to.

An old soldier of 1812, the eyes of the old
man kindle, and eagerly he listens to every detail, but even now we can see the quiet look of
the good, old mother; can see the weary eyes,
from whose pupils look a heart more weary, as
she gazes at that never-ending click, click, click
of the knitting-needles, but whose steadfast look
was not there, but far away with her four boys,
following the red battle-flag, one of whom, her
gallant baby boy, was so soon to be brought
home and laid away in a soldier's grave.

"We had the pleasure of a visit the last time
the Yankees were here," says his sister, "from a
Captain Van Horton, and he said that he knew
you."

"I know him," remarked Randolph. "What
of him ?"

"Oh, he came with a lot of tories, negroes,
mountain-cats and Yankees, and one of our
neighbors, hanging on to their troop, wanted to
take my mare, Bessie. Captain Van Horton was
good enough to prevent that. I have Bessie yet,
and the Yankees may get her, but the tories
never."

This sister, we will here inform the reader, had
lately married, and her home was upon a beautiful farm some five miles distant, and midway

between her father's place and the thriving village of G——.

A younger brother was in command of a battalion of cavalry, whose duty it was to patrol this very section, and, by consequence, the family was rather a thorn in the side of good Unionists.

Knowing his brother's dashing character, his handsome appearance, musical genius, and fondness of the society of the ladies, Randolph without hesitation asked, "Is Southey in danger of capture either by Yankees or by any of the fair damsels ?"

In a moment a cloud descended upon the group, as his mother calmly raises her eyes and answers, "That between 'that woman' and Captain Van Horton, Southey was not in a position to enjoy either his home or the society of ladies."

"But who is 'that woman?' and what has Van Horton to do with it?" interrogates Randolph.

"That woman, my son, is the daughter of the most honored gentleman of the county, our friend and neighbor; she is rather handsome, and intelligent, but it is all distorted by the intensity of her venom; her very being is absorbed with the one idea of hate and revenge."

"But I pray you tell me, mother, her haunts," said Randolph, in mimic fear, "that I may evade her poisoned shafts; and does she go armed?"

"Do not trifle, my son; you know the saying, that hell hath no fury like a woman scorned."

"Is that the matter? Who scorned her?" retorts Randolph.

"Your brother, Southey," answers his mother.

"Ah-h-h! There's where the shoe pinches," and Randolph relapses into a revery.

Click, click, click, goes the needles, and Randolph still is silent and in thought.

The day wanes, the soldier currys his horse, fills his trough with corn and his rack with fodder, and then goes to visit his mulatto mammy, to talk of times in Old Virginia when she bossed him, in his happy childhood days.

Seated upon her door-step, and enjoying the smoke from his old briar-root companion, Randolph asks:

"Aunt Rachel, it's rather quiet down here, is it not?"

"Well, mostly;" she answers, "but for the raiders—sometimes the Yankees, sometimes the robbers, and sometimes the Confederates. Between the three, we have trouble enough; and may the good Lord curse the wretches who stole my grave-clothes, all the most beautiful linen, all packed up and under my bed, when the Yankees raided here last, and they stole the lot. Thank God, old mistress saved her silver; for your sister Lucy put on a pair of Southey's pants and climbed the big tree over the house, and tied the things to top boughs and saved them.''

"Aunt Rachel," says Randolph, "tell me about brother Southey and 'that woman' mother spoke of, and about a Captain Van Horton, lately here,''

"Lor' honey, (with a chuckle) it is such a mix. You see 'that woman' is Miss F——, (you know her, of course you do), she is dead in love with Major Southey, and this Captain Van Horton and Miss F—— now are very great friends. You remember that big school-house in G——. It is said that Southey unexpectedly visits that school one day, was seen to leave in a very few moments, mount his horse and ride away like the wind. You know what a horseman he is; always at home on a horse's back. His troop passed some weeks later and he refused to recognize or return the salutation of Miss F——, and ordered your sister never to recognize her. Now, honey, you know it all. And oh, that woman's tongue! Since then she has circulated the lie that Southey was a coward!''

"No, it cannot be that the daughter of so good a father would stoop to slander," says Randolph.

"Yes, son, it is even so; but people here don't mind her lies, nor is she even respected any more; but abroad where she is not known, it might hurt, and moreover, she is breaking her old father's heart.''

Let us say right here, for the benefit of those who might expect the negro dialect, that Rachel is a true character, raised in the dwelling-house of her white people, partaking of their manners, customs and language, and in pride of family and respectful conduct would set a bright example for many of her unasked, unwanted and over-zealous sympathizers.

After a long and pleasant chat, Randolph rises.

With a kindly ''good-night, and may God bless you child,'' the old mammy closes her door, and Randolph retires to his room, thoughtful, sad, weary of body and of mind.

Two more days with the loved ones, and at early dawn of the fourth day he is mounted on the back of his gallant old charger, and with the warm kisses of affection still clinging to his lips, and the fervent prayer for God's good guidance on his journey of all the household, Randolph turns his horse's head towards the road, crosses the mountain, and directs his course up the romantic valley of the French Broad, intending to strike the railroad at Greenville, South Carolina. As he journeyed, troublesome thoughts of the loved ones at home and ''that woman,'' would crowd upon his mind, bringing worry and anxiety, and as the sequel proved, not without cause.

Chapter III.

COLUMBIA, South Carolina, was duly reached, and after a stay of two weeks, Randolph, with one hundred and fifty men, detailed from the camp near the city, bid adieu to the city and took the cars *en route* to the Army of Northern Virginia, then encamped around Fredericksburg, facing the army of General Hooker of Chancellorsville fame, and yclept Fighting Joe. Reporting to his chief, he was once again with his brother staff officers, exchanging the news of the trip for the gossip of the camp.

The long, lazy body of Captain Noble, a member of the staff, is observed to move, and with a half-awakened " Hello!" he chants his thoughts: " Lo! the lost sheep is gathered to its flock, and the shepherd rejoiceth, beholding the contents of his well-filled haversack, which the children of Jacobaster hath swung upon his neck. Say, Randolph, did you not remember our bowels, nor have compassion for the same, nor even remember in the days of thy youth and painful verdancy that the juice of corn—yea, even of the peach or apple, would please our palates, and cause our hearts to leap for joy?"

"Come, Noble," answers Randolph, " the sun may be held accountable for many changes in

nature, but I can swear that he never painted
your nose, nor can even the shadow of his
friendly eclipse hide its roseate shame. You
bear the evidence of your own conviction of
living too high, both in meat and drink.''

Noble shuts his eyes and groans out in mock
agony: ''He is lost! lost! gone clean astray;
been 'living too high,' and judges his betters by
himself;'' and quickly sitting up, he says, '' I will
bet the mess five to one that Randolph is fixed;
that he has a box and something good coming; open up the game, old boy, or I will give
you away, for I am the possessor of a message
for you from a—a—now who do you suppose?''

'' I know your propensity for schemes,'' answers Randolph; ''play honest, Noble, for I never
liked the word ' bribery.' ''

''My most obtusely verdant youth, and auto-
crat of the grub-box, keep on in the error of thy
ways, the fool is wise in his own conceit, and
when thou coolest, I will hearken unto thee; and,
further, I have taken charge, have concealed,
and preserved, one sweet, little missive from a
small village called Lexington, where thou did'st
strut and perspire, with sword and sash and a
high cock's feathers, as a valiant captain of Company B,'' and Noble, with a grand assumption
of dignity and nonchalance, quietly subsides.

'' I surrender,'' said Randolph; ''come fellows, all hands; I have a box, and in it a present of magnificent French brandy, just through the blockade, the pure stuff; it was given me by that generous patriot, Mr. Wagner, of the firm of Trenholm & Co., of Charleston, S. C.; he gave me, also, this elegant suit while in Columbia," and while the staff enjoyed the well-filled box of luxuries, Randolph read the following letter:

"LEXINGTON, VA., March 10, 186—.

"DEAR CAPTAIN: With all our woes, none seem so hard to bear as the suffering of our dear friends.

"You remember that on the 25th ult. your room-mate, Robert McKene, was to have been married to his long-loved sweetheart, Miss S——. News has reached us that he was killed at the head of his men, cheering them to repel a surprise. I know that you loved him well, for he was so true and brave, yet so gentle, and for this I suffer more, because I know how your heart will bleed. Poor Miss S—— is almost distracted with grief. May a merciful God bring comfort to a stricken heart, and teach her to trust to His mercy.

"Can you come and see us? We will be so happy to look upon your face once more.

"Wishing you all manner of good fortune in battle and in camp, I am, as ever, Your affectionate

MARGUERITE."

The first one of the three shot dead! The noise of the mess fell discordantly upon his ears; but with the sweet words of his best loved before his eyes, his mind was in part withdrawn from the contemplation of the loss of his friend, and just then the deep, sullen roar of a piece of artillery, as its echoing sound faintly died away, brought vividly to his mind the fact that they were soldiers, and a soldier had but to die when duty called.

With a heavy heart he joined the mess, and filling his glass, he turned to his brother officers, and with eyes bedimmed with tears, and a heart too full for utterance, he drank to the last drop in the glass.

"Did she saw you off, old boy?" questions Capt. Noble.

"Read!" answers Randolph, as he threw the note in their midst.

After reading, it was remarked by several that they were aware of the fact, many days before; that it was but the fate of war: "One of us may go to-morrow, still the army will march and counter-march, the flags will flutter as merrily in the breeze, and the war will go on all the same, and the dead forgotten."

So they descant upon the news, until the cheery voice of Captain Noble is heard saying:

"Cheer up, old man; you don't smoke, we do, so we'll destroy your weeds, while you imbibe. Attention! fill up, let joy abound! And now, Randolph, I will give you the promised message. Your friend, Lawrence Mayne, rode over from the 11th Virginia, and joined us in our magnificent repast—ménu: bread, coffee, meat. He wanted to see you bad, real bad; he seemed to be rather in the dumps, you know the dumps—upset, as it were. He says that he wants you to send a courier over to him to notify him as soon as you arrive. Now, save him a wee drop of that French soothing syrup, and you brace him up and save his soul.''

And with like chaff of the mess, the evening passes away, and one by one each rolls down his blanket, and the sullen boom of a Yankee gun, now and then, only mars the stillness of the night, but fails to disturb the slumbers of the staff around the tent of General R——.

The next day dawns brightly, and as soon as breakfast is finished a courier is sent to the camp of General G——, with the ''Compliments of Captain Randolph, and would Adjutant Mayne please call at the headquarters of General R——?''

The bugle was just sounding the dinner call when Adjutant Mayne entered Randolph's tent, with a smile upon his face, but oh! the sadness of that smile. Extending his hand, he says:

''Welcome! and the lost is found, and now we will kill the fatted calf, call in our gray-backed cherubs, and let us make merry. Tell us first the news of home, and of Marguerite; did you see her?''

"No, indeed," answers Randolph; "Cupid hides his bow when Mars issues his stern commands. Of home I am troubled."

Adjutant Mayne, speaking slowly, if not sadly, says:

"When you mentioned trouble I am reminded of the object of my visit, perhaps to further burden you. Hooker is across the river; our scouts tell us of the massing of men, as if the whole Yankee nation, with Europe, Asia and Africa to aid them, was enclosing us poor, hungry and ragged few in its embrace; and before we 'mix' with them I want to talk with you, as we did when 'rats' in old No. 17 at the V. M. I."

"Go on, Lawrence; I am all attention," answers Randolph.

Mayne asks: "Do you remember that fellow Van Horton?"

Randolph nods affirmatively.

"Well," continues Mayne, "that man is not of this country at all, but a miserable importation from Europe, and is both robber and spy; under the garb of a Federal captain when playing soldier, and Mr. Hobson as spy."

"Really, you astonish me!" answers Randolph. "Where do you get your information?"

"An exchanged prisoner brought me a note from dear little Sadie," answers the adjutant, telling me of the impostor and scoundrel; that her father, knowing his disreputable character, has requested his absence from his house, and that she had admired his fine appearance, but never loved, and now despised him; that she was my own little sweetheart, and by the help of friends and gold, was coming down to the home of Marguerite to be in easy reach, where I could visit her when duty allowed. Now, isn't that delighful?"

"Yes, it is delighful," answers Randolph, "but what has that to do with the long face that you are wearing?"

"Oh! now you have me; it is so good of her, the sweet little Yankee darling, to leave home and friends, and come away here in this starving country, for what? Only to see me. It is so much happiness, that it seems unnatural, and it oppresses me, and I fear, yes and even tremble lest I shall lose it."

After thus speaking, Adjutant Mayne seems absorbed in gloomy forebodings.

"Look here, Mayne," says Randolph, "you are dyspeptic." Noble, and all the mess in fact, foresaw the need of a tonic, and the same is now provided, and by the help of my right bower, the Jack of Spades, we will proceed to test the efficacy of the dose. "Here Jack, you black rascal!" (a trim young negro appears); "bring fresh water and two glasses. Now,

Lawrence, here's a health to all good lassies, and our's especially; down she goes."

"Randolph, do you ever see the dark side of anything?"

"The clown must keep the audience merry, if his darling babe lies at home dying in its mother's arms," answers Randolph: "and I advise you further to brace up, and if fortune or misfortune puts the robber or spy into our possession, we will not have to look very far for a halter."

As the word "halter" is spoken, a small and slender young man, with a bright face, with light hair, and dressed in the uniform of an artillery officer, suddenly appears before the two speakers, and curtly asks: "Who wants a halter? I have plenty for such work, and may have use for less in a day or two."

The speaker is Captain Pelham, already known to fame, and an ex-cadet of the V. M. I.

"Why," says Randolph, "what's up?"

"Don't you know," goes on Pelham, "that Hooker has crossed the river, both the Rapidan and Rappahannock, and is in Chancellorsville, and is fortifying? I saw Old Stonewall and Massa Bob hobnobbing awhile ago, and we'll hear the music of the brass band before many hours. You both are in it, for you both are with Rodes, and he and Stonewall are too much alike not to

D A—3

be first in the fray. But I am in a hurry; just stopped in to give you a hint. Load up.''

"We have, in another way, and have a charge for you. Come, stand in, and here's to victory!''

This announcement put an end to further conversation, and the friends separate in quest of further news. Pelham goes straight to meet Averill at Kelly's Ford and drive him back, and then to give up his young life, a sacrifice upon the altar of his country on that memorable 17th day of March, 1863.

The days roll by, but now all is bustle and hurry; the couriers flash by on errands of haste; long lines of veterans clad in gray, with bayonets glistening in the sun, stand in readiness for the conflict; now and then is heard the sharp report of the picket as he cautiously feels the way for the masses in blue behind him, and high above all is the roar of the big guns; for on this 29th day of April, 20,000 Federal troops have crossed the Rappahannock River, and now threaten the right and rear of Lee's army at Hamilton's Crossing. This effort at a diversion falls a flat failure, for Lee well knows that the bulk of the Yankee army is at Chancellorsville and well entrenched.

If it was the inspiration of Hooker to attract attention to the Confederate right, and then to move out of his fortified stronghold upon Lee's

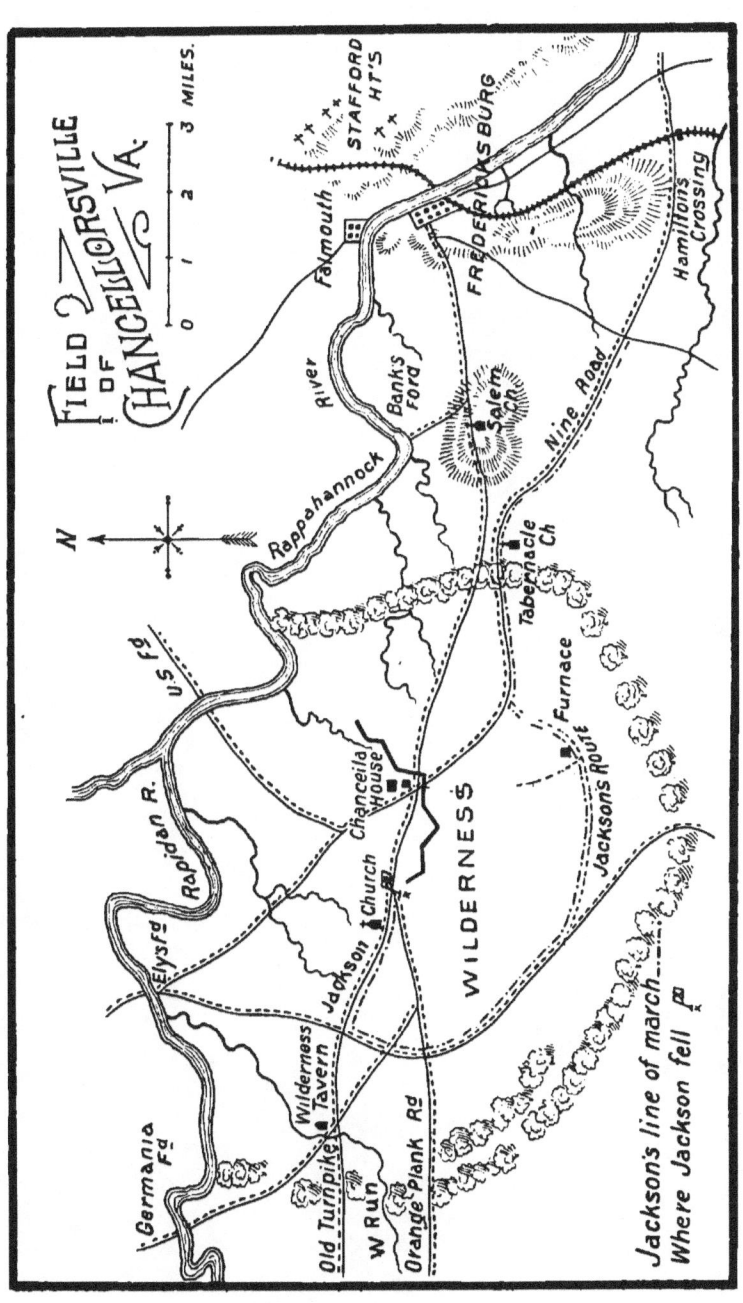

FIELD OF CHANCELLORSVILLE VA.

0 1 2 3 MILES.

N

STAFFORD HT'S

FREDERICKSBURG

Hamiltons Crossing

Falmouth

Nine Road

Banks Ford

Salem Ch

Rappahannock River

Tabernacle Ch

Furnace

U.S. Fd

Jacksons Route

Rapidan R.

Chancellor House

WILDERNESS

Elys Fd

Jackson Church

Germania Fd

Wilderness Tavern

Old Turnpike

W Run

Orange Plank Rd

Jackson's line of march........
Where Jackson fell ⚔

left, and to double up his army and crush it, or drive it into the river by the sheer force of his masses, perhaps, acting upon the old maxim, *similia similibus curantur*, caused Lee to put into execution the tactics so feebly undertaken by his opponent.

Leaving one division of Jackson's corps to watch the movement of the 20,000 under General Sedgewick, Lee hurries with Jackson, who, moving the three remaining divisions of his corps, namely: Rodes, A. P. Hill and Colston, which joining Anderson, already at the Tabernacle Church, five miles from Chancellorsville, proceed to "attack and repulse the enemy," as per order of the Commander-in-Chief.

Anderson with his command, as gallant and true and steady as the Old Guard of Napoleon, deploy with their faces towards Chancellorsville, and sweep forward to meet the trained regulars of the United States army, under Sykes, and force them back, with all their vaunted prowess, to the music of that "rebel yell" which had quickened the pulses and oftener the heels of the blue-coated soldiery, from the First Manassas down to the present time.

Jackson, throwing forward to Anderson's relief the four brigades of Lane, Heth, Ramsour and McGowan, continued to press the enemy back until reaching the enemy's first line of intrenchments, which had been masked until reached, owing to the density of the growth of timber; and finding the day far spent, a halt was called, and the army was bivouacked about two miles from Chancellorsville. In the short time the Federal forces had occupied Chancellorsville they had shown an activity, energy and enterprise, thoroughly in keeping with their universally accorded reputation of go-aheadativeness, but betraying by their beaver-like energy of turning up the earth, felling trees, planting abattis, etc., that "protection" was the desideratum, and the cutting off of Lee's retreat when so ceremoniously "bagged," the airy dream of a newly fledged "Correspondent."

Many a jolly Confederate veteran wondered at the magnitude of labor performed by soldiers who had the world to feed them, and the world to replenish their shattered ranks. To cut off the line of Confederate retreat, General Hooker had very thoughtfully, for the emergency of an assault from the direction of Fredericksburg, by a double line of works in the shape of two sides of a rectangle, one side running north and south and facing Fredericksburg, and crossing the main road between the two places, and the other side perpendicular to it facing south, with front to the timber called The Wilderness, and its rear parallel to the river. In a council of war it was decided upon, on the part of the Confederates, that by reason of the impregnability of Hooker's position and the disparity of forces, a front attack should be abandoned, and more especially from motives of humanity.

But a man was there who never turned his back when a fight was on, and Stonewall Jackson, the stern old warrior, whose frown was a volume of reproof, and whose smile stole the heart and cheered the soul as a rift of sunshine through the clouds of despair, was the man to solve the problem.

A narrow, crooked and unkept by-road debouched to the left, hedged in by an interminable growth of vines, pines and scrub-oak, winding westwardly, then northerly, then westwardly again till the old Brock road is reached. By this route and a night march the Man of Menassas proposed to flank the Federal Hooker and solve the problem of "cutting off a line of retreat."

Thus, while one portion of the army under Lee slept, Jackson at break of day, with Rodes in front, followed by A. P. Hill's and Colston's divisions, was on the march through the thicket of The Wilderness, with the accompaniment only of their own foot-falls, and the melancholy calls of the whip-poor-wills, who seem to have especially colonized this gloomy thicket.

Arriving at the Furnace, and while placing a

regiment in position to guard an approach from a by-road from Chancellorsville to that point, our old friend Randolph meets Adjutant Mayne, and after greetings they were discussing the chances of the hazardous movement, when their attention is suddenly attracted to a courier, who, dashing up, hands General Jackson a note, and with cap in hand awaits his orders.

"That's General Stuart's courier," says Randolph, "now watch."

The note being read, Jackson raises his head; there is a kindling of the eye, the faintest trace of a smile, and a curt, "Thanks, my compliments to General Stuart; that will do sir."

And replacing his cap, the courier rides back to his command.

"Ah! ha! see that?" says Randolph, "you know old Jack too long to be unable to read the answer to the question; if we don't give them a 'side wipe' after Jackson's most improved style, I'm a tinker." And now having reached the Brock road, they make better progress, and coming in sight of the cavalry, they passed Jackson and Stuart on an elevation, glasses in hand, examining the enemy's right flank and rear.

Knowing that every man now should be at his post, Randolph bids his old friend "au revoir," and jestingly adds, "we'll drive them across the

creek and win a furlough, and then we'll go together to see—you know who, my lad. The
Lord be with you."

Adjutant Mayne, looking him steadily in the
face, with a solemnity as unusual as it was inexpressible, simply answered, "Amen!"

And now the time is come. Rodes' division
is deployed; six hundred feet behind comes A.
P. Hill's, a similar space is Colston's division,
both the latter in column. As fast as the men
can penetrate the thicket they advance upon the
unsuspecting troops of the Federal left flank.

At fifteen minutes past 5 o'clock Jackson let
slip his dogs of war, and if the eager hunter
chased faster or a more demoralized quarry, he
or they are entitled to the blue ribbon, over all
past and present lovers of the chase.

The men of Rodes burst upon the unsuspicious German troops of Howard, the noted Eleventh Corps of Sigel, who incontinently lost their
suppers, and with the joyous "rebel yell," and
the quickning crash of musketry and artillery,
so utterly disorganized and demoralized were
they, that losing their heads, they rushed head-
long to the rear, crashing into trees, reckless of
everything in front, but determined to flee from
the wrath behind.

Soon Hill and Colston came up, to add to the
enthusiasm, and all went over the enemy's

works, carrying confusion badly confounded to the flying Dutch; and now mingled with the rush of men, were the maddened rush of riderless and uncontrolled horses, battery wagons, ambulances, gun-carriages, caissons—some flying, some overturned, many poor brutes in harness struggling in the helpless agony of death, either by shot or collision—all, all one inextricable mass of frightened men and brutes.

Whole regiments ran without firing a gun, throwing away their guns to facilitate their speed; madly seeking safety from the wrath of the yelling Reb.

Batteries, in their mad haste, crashed against tree or stump, were captured, and turned upon the fleeing mob.

Who could paint with pen or brush the awful stampede of that day, so as to portray to the man of to-day the awful terror of the fleeing, and the reckless chase for life and safety.

On, on came the yelling Confederates, planting their volleys upon the backs of flying men, even in solid column.

With the incessant volleys of Confederate musketry, men, horses, wagons and all the paraphernalia of war were jumbled into such an inextricable confusion that it seemed a panorama of pandemonium, upon the fields of Hades, with all the aroma of its sulphurous canopy. In

THE ROUT AT CHANCELLORSVILLE.

a word, as expressed by a Northern writer, '' the stampede was universal, the disgrace general.''

Until 8 o'clock p. m. the route continued to a point, where a ridge was occupied, one-half mile from Hooker's stronghold at the Chancellor House.

Our two young officers, whom we left about to go into action from the Brock road, were with their respective commands. and though going into the battle in different divisions, found themselves together again, by the intermingling of the different commands, being so intent in their enthusiasm, that discipline gave place to ardor, and for this intermingling, together with the darkness, a halt was called.

If Jackson, like Joshua of old, could have called a halt of the sun for two short hours, the Sixteenth Army Corps of Hooker would have had a shorter and a different history to record.

Our young friends met cordially, and were exchanging the commonplace greetings and congratulations of so successful a move, when Mayne was called away to carry a message to General Jackson. In the gloom of the trees, he was pointed out the direction of his search, and after many pulls and rubs of vines and boughs, he came near the person of the General, when, without any warning, or any conceivable object, the gloom lighted up with a heavy volley fired

from the Confederate infantry. Adjutant Mayne
fell badly wounded, with him many others, and
oh! sad day for the Confederacy, he, the idol
of the army, at last lay crushed by the rifles of
his own troops!

The pride of a glorious victory vanished from
the white faces of his gallant men, and oh! the
wail that went up from the hearts of soldiers,
and from thousands at the hearths of their
Southern homes.

With the left arm of Jackson went the strength
of the right arm of Lee; with his life went the
hopes of thousands for future success; but with
his life as he spent it, his deeds as he wrought
them, his patriotism, piety and glory, all will
stand out in history, in all time, as a shining
example of virtue, honor and heroism.

At dawn the next morning, Bob, the darkey
henchman of Mayne, came to Randolph at the
outposts, and with tears and lamentations, tells
him that his master's horse was caught with
bloody saddle, and that he was now hitched near
the hospital at the intersection of the old turnpike and the Germania plank road; that no
one would answer him, and that he "knowed
nuffin'."

Sending the boy back to the hospital, Randolph followed with many misgivings. As he
rode back over the field, hundreds of dead bodies

of men and horses encumbered the ground, literally strewed with every appliance of war, which could be supplied by a government enriched by a war of oppression and plunder.

His mind oppressed with unwelcome thoughts, Randolph found himself involuntarily repeating that parting word, Amen; and lifting his eyes discovered the ubiquitous Bob running towards him, and with a sickly display of white teeth, saying: "I found him, sir! hurt bad and wants you. I told him you was a-coming."

Arriving at the hospital, Bob takes his horse, and Randolph enters a shed-room near where Jackson lies in mortal agony.

Upon an improvised bed, made of straw, and covered with an army blanket, Randolph finds his comrade; his pale face with closed eyes, his blood-stained uniform meet his gaze. Approaching closer he tenderly lifts the hand of Mayne, when their eyes meet in mutual love and sympathy; no words pass their lips, only a gentle pressure of the hands, and the stillness is only interrupted by the gentle tread of the surgeons and their assistants hurriedly attending their anxiously awaiting patients. The services of the surgeon performed, he administers a simple narcotic, and the frown begotten of pain slowly disappears from the patient's face, and sweet sleep, now so near the cousin of death, clasps the soldier in its dreamy embrace. While Randolph gently bathes his feverish brow and moistens his lips, the surgeon tells him that Mayne's wounds bear the signature and seal of Death; that they are beyond the control of a surgeon's art.

Sleep brings life a short reprieve, and the sufferer asks to telegraph to Lexington and see if Sadie had come, and if so, to come without delay to Fredericksburg, to the old Marye mansion, to which he begs to be taken. The surgeon makes no objection, and Randolph hurries away to obey.

Returning eastwardly, he finds Hooker beaten back across the Rappahannock, the woods still smoking, where the wounded and the dead were caught in its cruel grasp on the day succeeding Jackson's wound, and pushing on, found Lee driving Sedgwick back in confusion across his pontoons at Banks' Ford; and in a gloomy rain sat himself down to await the answer to his dispatch.

After long, weary hours the welcome message came: "LEXINGTON, May 7, 1863.
"*Capt. Phil. Randolph,*

        "*Care Gen. R. E. R., Fredericksburg, Va.:*
  "We start immediately; meet us at train.

                        "MARGUERITE."

Mounting his horse, Randolph returns with an ambulance, and twelve hours later his friend is, after a tedious trip, resting in the house whose name is a synonym of valor and virtue in the home circles of Fredericksburg and in the command in which the name has served.

In the quietness of the evening, the old Marye mansion looks over the town, now rent and torn by shot and shell, but within its walls, there hovers a spirit whose restlessness, expressed in long drawn sighs, quick and eager scanning of the door, tell of an unquietness born of a knowledge that certain things have a certain limit, and that limit is final and unalterable.

Trains have a schedule, but "military necessity" side-tracks and holdovers disorder the best regulated; and after hours of impatient waiting, inquiries unnoticed, or unanswered, a long whistle is heard, and a train comes in with its wheezy, overworked engine. But horror of horrors! in the box cars are huddled infantrymen, whose heads are poked out of every available hole, and who chaff every one without regard to color, rank or previous condition.

About to turn away in despair, two ladies are observed to step from a rear coach, which is attached for the accommodation of the commissioned officers, and a figure but too well known not to be identified at such a distance, causes Captain Randolph to hasten to their side, if not to comfort, at least to lessen the weight of affliction.

Little is said, but Randolph in his effort to gently prepare Sadie for the meeting desired, by tone and action betrays his knowledge, but his strong arm supports the drooping form till the threshold is passed and the outstretched arms of poor Mayne clasp the form of her he had lovéd so long and well, and the little head, still crowned with the wealth of sunny curls, is hidden on his neck, and with throbbing heart and aching temples she pours out her thoughts in a torrent of loving words.

"Tut, tut!" interposes good Doctor Murdock: "don't murder my patient with kindness. Come, ladies; I am prepared for you; I know that you are hungry and tired. Let your maid bring your sachels. A little rest for you and my patient, and upon good behavior you shall have him all to yourselves."

With a happy smile, Mayne, growing steadily weaker, sinks into a profound slumber, and as Randolph sits by his side, with the faithful Bob, he watches and notes the ominous, faint, quick breathing, and as night creeps on he discovers by the mantel clock that it is past the hour of midnight; that Bob is dead asleep, and that he is almost nodding. The faintest sound of a footstep startles him. Was he dreaming? But drifting again toward dreamland, again he is aroused as if by the opening of a door. Feeling

no anxiety, his pistols being near by upon the
table at his side, he picked up a book, and had
just opened to read, when again he surely heard
a door open. Looking over the book—was he
dreaming, or was it a spirit? Neither; for there
stood Sadie, clad in a robe of soft blue material,
with cuffs and neck trimmed with narrow lace,
the beautiful neck exposed, clear and white as
marble. She moved toward the wounded man
softly with her slippered feet, her eyes wide open,
but bent upon the floor. Gently kneeling by the
bedside of her lover, she clasped her hands, and
bent her head, in the position of earnest, heart-
broken supplication; the lips moved, but no
word escaped the lips. Suddenly the maid hastily entered, and took the sleeper in her arms as
a mother would her babe and disappeared, leaving Randolph still wondering and alone with his
sleepers.

The door had scarcely closed behind the
women, when an opposite door, opening upon
the main hall, was gently opened and a man,
seemingly of middle age, in the garb of an ordi-
nary countryman, stood before Randolph. With
a nod and a scrape of the foot he remarked that
he "supposed this a tavern."

"You will correct your supposition by retiring
immediately," Randolph remarked.

"Well," he answered, "curiosity will git the

advantage of folks; but, I thought that I might find some acquaintances; and, stranger, it 'pears like I knowed you, and might know your folks.''

Fearing that he would awaken the sleeper, Randolph advanced towards the intruder unarmed, and when near enough to lay his hand upon him, the stranger quietly placed the muzzle of a revolver to his head, saying: ''I am Mr. Van Horton, at your service. I came up on the same train with Sadie. As Mayne is dying, I will not kill him. I will remember you to your brother, whom I shall meet,'' and with a curse for Sadie, backed out into the night, and left Randolph trembling with rage, and stupefied by the suddenness of the unwelcome apparition.

Morning broke clear and bright, and early came the girls, and soon the kind doctor, with a happy word of comfort for all.

Randolph spoke no word of the night, nor was the adventure of the sleep-walker mentioned.

Sadie, with all the loving care of a mother, bathed the face and hands of her lover, smoothed his hair and softly kissed his lips, and placing her chair so as to face him, took his hand, clasping it within her two.

''Now, tell me, dearest, how you feel?''

''Weaker,'' he answers; ''notice my voice. Ah! sweetheart, I dreamed of you last night.''

Breathing a long-drawn sigh, he continues: "We were to be married, when the black face of Van Horton came between us; suddenly, Randolph, indignant at his action, slew him like a dog; 'twas only a dream; but you were mine, even for the brief moment."

More faintly, he adds: "Oh! Sadie, if I could only live to love you, to go back with you to the old hills of Rockbridge, where we first met, and where we first learned to love."

Poor Sadie is speechless, and with tearful eyes and agonized heart, drinks in the words that may be the last upon earth.

Feverishly, he continues: "You will think of me, dear, and come to see the sod that covers a heart always true to one little Yankee worth all the treasures of earth, and the adoration of a worthier heart than mine"—and for the first time he tries to raise up, but, grasping at the empty air, he groans most sadly. Only a shudder, and all is still.

The patient doctor, standing near, bids Sadie say farewell. Clasping her arm around his neck with all the reckless abandon of love lost, she kisses lips, cheek and brow, murmuring: "Good-bye, love, good-bye!" until Marguerite, who has been a suffering but patient witness, leads her away.

D A—4

CHAPTER IV.

A FURLOUGH to accompany the dead, enables Randolph once more to visit his family, now living in the village of G——, already mentioned; their home having been totally destroyed by tory robbers. Striking across the mountains, he turns his horses' head westward. The air is cool, and the May days are cheerful in the bright garments of leaf and flowers of Spring, while the now unhunted birds sweep before and around him in notes made sweeter, no doubt, from a sense of greater security from fright and pursuit. At home on horseback, Randolph rides not hurriedly, because next to self—his horse; they have ate, slept and suffered together; and now as it grows dark he approaches a neat country residence, and riding to the gate utters a loud hallo! and is answered by a female voice, bidding him to alight and come in, with a cordiality native to Old Virginia.

Observing the lady's sleeves rolled up, and believing that his arrival had disturbed her, perhaps in the discharge of some domestic occupation, Randolph courteously apologized for the inopportune interruption and begged forgiveness, when the lady smilingly told him that his anxiety was wholly unnecessary and uncalled for, as she was only doctoring one of "Lee's miserables," and if he wasn't too tired, that he could come in and help.

Actuated more by curiosity than by any desire to help, Randolph followed the lady to a room, and there found the object of her attention. A brawny, manly looking soldier, lay upon the bed, whose sheets, as white as snow, made a vivid contrast with the dirty, gray pants, the old ragged shirt and heelless socks of the man lying flat upon his face.

A negro man stood near, holding a basin of water, and the soldier's shirt being split open in the back, exposed a large bandage pasted to his back, bloody and dirty from long use—this was the panorama exhibited Randolph upon entering the room.

"Excuse me, Mr. Ruke," remarks the hostess, "I have hastened back as soon as possible."

"'Tis all right, madam; but pardon me, O'Rourke is me name, and was the name of me father before me," and turning his face to one side and towards Randolph, after a cool survey, he adds, "Chancellorsville," emphasizing by reversing his arm and sticking out his thumb towards the bloody bandage.

As a cavalryman, in a charge under Fitz Lee,

a fragment of shell had torn a large flesh wound in his back, which had secured him a furlough, and he was now on his way home, on Randolph's very route.

The good woman, with much sponging succeeded in removing the old bandage, and carefully cleansing the wound and making the necessary applications, at last pronounced the words of satisfactory relief and accomplishment, "*there*, and don't you feel better?"

"May the blessed angels keep you, lady," says O'Rourke. "Howly Mother! it is like a bird I'm afther failing, and if me shoes had better soles, I'd dance for your diversion an Irish jig that would astonish the queen's own cook; and spaking of the cook, I am not so tired as I am hungry. Master Bob is a foine fighter, but as a feeder, he can't draw mutton where there is no sheep, nor beef where there is no cattle. And, madam, have you a bit of a strap, for the cart that I rode up here upon jolted out the very blood and breath of me body, and me waistband has grown six inches, or me waist has shrunk seven, an' galluses I must have; and by the powers of Howly Mary me very teeth are loose entirely."

This harangue held the lady in speechless wonder, and turning to one side, she threw open the door to the dining-room, displaying a well-served table, shining invitingly in the light of the lamps.

Mr. O'Rourke's face was wreathed in smiles, and so intent was his eyes upon the table that, not heeding the doorstep, he came near sprawling upon the floor.

Strange to say, Randolph had stumbled upon an aunt of Marguerite, as he found out through Mr. O'Rourke's incessant talk of the late battle, and the "murtherin scoundrel" who fired that bloody shell (needless to·say the one that struck Mr. O'Rourke), and knowing the relations existing between Randolph and her niece, also of Mayne and Sadie, at her request Randolph told in detail of the last rites of sepulture to his deceased friend in the cemetery of his family in Lynchburg, of the trip with Marguerite and Sadie to their home in Rockbridge, and his short visit, made so by the grief of one and the sympathy of the other.

After a refreshing rest, on the next day, O'Rourke having secured an old cavalry Rosinante, Randolph bids his hostess a thankful adieu, in which O'Rourke joins, with many hopes of meeting again, without any lessening in the future of individual shadows, they once more journey west.

O'Rourke proves to be an agreeable companion and a fearless, dare-devil soldier. In his right hand he swings a sturdy hickory stick, which is a pointer for objects of his notice, a propeller for his steed, a sabre for the cavalry-man, and a shillalah for the Son of Erin.

Mr. O'Rourke sings, too, but while his voice is strong, it is not sweet, and his tunes run from one line of "Lorena" to another in "The old grey hoss come a-rushin' froo de wilderness."

On one occasion the word "Wilderness" seemed to revive some recollections of Mr. O'Rourke, and he asks: "And, Cap., do you mind that bloody bush in The Wilderness? How in the devil the boys got through it wid their clothes on! The horse and meself were hung up, tripped up or down, and I was just enjoying meself when I felt the stroke in me back."

"Don't repeat that any more, O'Rourke," says Randolph; "but tell me, did you leave the heels of your socks at Chancellorsville?"

"No, begorra; but I left skin enough to patch them," he answers, laughing loudly and joyously at his own misfortunes.

Many miles had been ridden, long hours had passed, and after a profound silence, interrupted only by the hoof-falls of the horses, O'Rourke slowly arouses from his seeming apathy, and as with the sudden birth of an unusual thought, asks:

"And, Captain, is it married you are?"

"I am not so fortunate as yet," he answers.

"But you have a gir-rul, I am after thinking," retorts O'Rourke.

"And why do you think so, pray?" asks Randolph. "Do I sigh and sing love-songs in your presence, or talk in my sleep?"

"My experience," says O'Rourke, "about the sighing and singing is limited, but sure you must have a slight cross of the Yankee, whin you make a guess; for in your slape last night you called 'Marguerite!' and unless she's your sister, bedad she must be your gir-rul;" and a laugh with the ring and force of true enjoyment follows the unfolding of the burden of last night's discovery.

Unable to control his feelings and his surprise, and blushing to his brows, Randolph tells him of his betrothed; and having exhausted his theme, has unexpectedly excited a feeling of sympathy in the breast of the sturdy soldier, which begets a desire upon the part of O'Rourke to pour into the ears of his superior his own marital troubles.

"I have meself some expariance in the matrimonial market; Oi'm married," drawls O'Rourke, in a meditative mood.

"Indeed; let me congratulate you—"

"Sh—top, Captain, if yer plase," cries O'Rourke; "I've a wee bit to tell ye. I was on the Aist Tinnessee and Virginny railroad worruk-in' on a fill in a beautiful valley. Close to our shanty ould man Dobbins had as swate a little farrum as iver yer eyes was laid upon. Sure it was a divarsion to survey the primises; and afther buthermilk, as an excuse, I wint to the house, and making noise enough with the help of the flop-eared house dogs to scare a banshee, there came to the dure as swate a lass as iver blessed the eyes of man. I got the buthermilk and a fluttering under me jacket, and all night long I dreamed of buthermilk and the darling Kitty of the Dobbins' house. Howly Moses! I was struck!

"My ould folks ran the boarding shanty on the worruk, close by, and with the hilp of the ould lady, who was a grate admirer of the farrum, if the gir-rul was a Protestant, we were married, and a jolly jubilee it was. And we were gitting along pretty well up to the breaking out of the war. The ould man Dobbins and his wife were Union, Kitty and I Secesh. Sometimes the Yankees would overrun us, thin we were all Union; thin the Confiderates would swarm upon us, in that avint we were all Confiderates; it was the tormint of our lives, but it kept pace in the family. But worse was to come, and the divil's own hand in it. Kitty she gits converted. As long as she was not converted into a nagur or a

Yankee, I didn't moind it. Well, thin, up she goes and enlists in the Baptist Church, for the war, I suppose.

"You know, and maybe you don't, but my folks are Roman Catholics, and I am naythur Catholic nor Baptist.

"The ould wimmin began it, and the young ones jined in afther the ould ones got out of breath entirely. Sure it was religion, the praist and the parson they were rowing over. The very bones of me ache whin I think of it. There was Kitty's Ma and my Ma, and the rest of the wimmin, and sure it is, I heard more of infant baptism, immersion, conversion, subversion, falling from grace, of Howly Mary, Father Riley and Pastor Parker, until I was crazy wid the talk. I didn't know a divil of a word what version was best, whether Riley's or Parker's, or whither it was disgrace or afther grace they were at; and for six long wakes it was the tormint of me life.

"Divil of a word I iver said, or they would have, ivery one of thim, been upon the top of me back. But for the whisky hid in the straw they would have been the death of me. But it was no use; the battle over the infants, the water howly and unhowly, got worse and more of it, till me ould friend, Dennis McKelsey, came along going to the war, and mounting my horse, I jined him for Master Bob and the army."

Having reached a commanding point in the road, Randolph interrupts further discourse of O'Rourke, by pointing out in the distance the steeples and housetops in the village of G——, Tenn., now only a few miles distant. Soon Randolph is once more in the arms of his parents, and enjoying the verbal as well as culinary blessings of Mammy Rachel.

From her he learns that Van Horton has suddenly disappeared; "that woman" Miss F— is reported engaged or married to him, and still unceasingly annoys and persecutes his brother with slanderous innuendoes, even worries his innocent sister; and worse still, her maliciousness has extended to his mother and father; for the the fiendish followers of Van Horton drove his father barefooted in a chill winter night, and tore down his very dwelling from over the heads of his wife and daughter, and deliberately fired upon his aged and defenceless mother. He learns also that his brother, Southey, came up with his command and retalliated upon several of the robber gang, and made things lively for awhile, and now, like wild animals at bay, they stand glaring at one another, and God only knows what next will turn up.

Randolph hears enough to make him wish for peace, for the sake of the old folks at home; but deep down in his bosom there dwells a desire for vengeance. How often in this life does it appear that a special Providence protects the designing wretch who is brutally reckless of every principle of right, of virtue and of honor!

Not many days elapse before Mr. O'Rourke and Rosinante appear, considerably mended and improved, and once more, adieu to home and family and on the road to camp and to duty.

CHAPTER V.

AFTER a long and tedious journey, our travelers reach Staunton, where O'Rourke disappears in search of his command, and Randolph eagerly seeks his own.

All was bustle and confusion of men in every style of conveyance, as well as footmen, eagerly pressing up the Valley, for the Army of Northern Virginia has crossed the Potomac, bent upon the invasion of Yankee soil, hitherto ignorant of the terrors of war.

Fortunate in finding an ambulance, Randolph joined Major P——, a gallant officer of the artillery, and rapidly drove to overtake the advancing army.

Learning that Ewell had crossed the Potomac at Williamsport, they hurried to that point, and crossing, saw the first evidences of the advance fighting in the many dead horses scattered upon the banks of the canal.

After resting their tired horses, they pushed on to Chambersburg, and passed through the rear guard, being Pickett's brigade, and found Col. Stuart, an old V. M. I. professor, in command of the place. Here, for the first time during the war, Randolph finds and feels himself upon the enemy's soil. Soldiers in gray are scattered over the streets, merely chaffing some of the young ladies of the place, who, in the excess of their loyalty, display from their bosoms miniature specimens of the stars and stripes.

Standing at the head of an alley, and in front of a small two-story brick edifice, over whose door was written BANK, Randolph notes across the street some of these ladies so decorated passing through a jolly, loitering group of Hood's Texans, when a long-suffering Johnnie observes, rather in the manner of conferring knowledge for the good and benefit of the decorated, that his command had the unwholesome reputation of storming *breastworks* when flying the Federal flag. No answering reparte came from the addressed.

No disorder occurred in the village; no act of outrage or oppression occurred during Randolph's stay of sixteen hours.

He has, however, one remembrance of the head of that alley. Hearing footsteps descending the stairway of that bank, he turned and feasted his eyes upon a handsome young lady, evidently the daughter of an official of the bank; but oh! how short-lived his happiness, for with a toss of her fair, young head, and an ominous elevation of the lips and the tip of her nose, she turned for his view and edification a rear elevation, which he admired, of course; but from the lady's pantomimic exhibition, he was left under a most disagreeable apprehension that it was either the new gray suit he wore, or the odor of the naughty joke across the street that caused the facial disturbance and the sudden disposition to "about face."

There were no improper liberties taken, nor unjust indignities imposed upon the citizens, and Randolph, in company with one of the best known and most gallant artillery officers, spent the night in the straw of a stable-loft upon this very same alley aforesaid.

On the morning of July 1st he again enters the ambulance and starts northward, towards Carlisle, where they proposed to overtake the command of General Rodes. Going three miles, they ran into a skirmish between Confederate cavalry and Yankee home guards. They were thus turned back to Chambersburg, and drove thence rapidly on the national pike straight for Gettysburg.

About 4 o'clock p. m. they arrived at Cashtown, and here was found the headquarters train of Randolph's division.

After greeting his old companions, he rode out to the main road, where Gettysburg, about five miles distant, could be distinctly seen; the lines of the contending troops also were plainly visible.

The Federal lines were being driven rapidly back towards Gettysburg, and Randolph was again viewing the men of Rodes repeating the performance of Chancellorsville—chasing the Eleventh corps of Yankee Dutch hirelings, not only from the field, but to and through the streets of Gettysburg.

Night fell, the Confederates victorious at every point; the Federals broken and disorganized, their trains driving to the rear, and stragglers without number going the same way. The men of Lee, worn out by long marches, laid down upon their arms and slept.

All night long fresh Federal troops were arriving, and those who had been running turned back when it was discovered that none pursued.

When morning dawned, the two armies had about mustered their strength, and were busily engaged in disposing of batteries and brigades in designated positions.

The Confederates were disposed as follows: Ewell's line in and through Gettysburg, extending east and west and facing south; A. P. Hill on his right, his line running north and south on Seminary Ridge and parallel to Willoughby Run and facing east, with Longstreet on his right on the same line, and facing the same direction.

Round Top Mountain, on Longstreet's extreme right, rose like a huge sentinel guarding the Federal left flank, while the spurs and ridges trending off to the north of it afforded unrivalled positions for the use of artillery.

The puffs of smoke rising at intervals along the line of hills as the Federal batteries fired upon such portions of our line as became exposed to view, clearly showed that these advantages had not been neglected.

The thick woods, which in great part covered the sides of Round Top and the adjacent hills, concealed from view the rugged nature of the ground, which increased four-fold the difficulties of the attack.

Little Round Top was in front of Longstreet's center, and Devil's Den about a quarter of a mile nearer to him, and about midway between Big and Little Round Top.

About 5 o'clock p. m., Longstreet's right swept forward, and after desperate fighting carried these points—desperate hand-to-hand fighting being displayed on both sides. At the same time a portion of Ewell's corps charged the Federal forces before the cemetery, driving them off and capturing their guns, and even reaching Evergreen cemetery, the stronghold of the enemy's right; but for want of co-operation the movement failed, as did Longstreet's, both failures being the result more from lack of sufficient force. Nevertheless, night found the advantage accruing to Lee's army, with Ewell in *statu quo*, and Longstreet and Hill closed up on the Federal left. Another night to add to a position naturally strong, to add to their force and replenish their munitions of war, and Lee many miles from his base of supplies and with nearly exhausted caissons.

But there was one thing which could be truly said without boasting—that the Army of Northern Virginia knew how to fight and die, but they knew not what it was to be whipped.

The next day, the 3d of July, dawned brightly. A spirit of quietude pervaded both armies, until about the hour of 2 p. m., Randolph, being upon the crest of Seminary Ridge, about two or three hundred yards south of the National pike, heard two heavy guns fired in quick succession. In a moment there responds a crash of artillery, the brazen voice of one hundred and fifty pieces, answered promptly by as many more, together with the hurtling of shot and shell, created a vision of awe-inspiring grandeur seen but seldom in a lifetime, and once seen never forgotten.

In a twinkling the heavens are obscured; a black cloud hangs overhead, and looking up,

D A—5

there flashes here and there in the sulphurous canopy the lurid fire of varied shapes and sizes, but looking straight to the front and across the valley, the flames seem to rush from the muzzles of the field-pieces many feet in length.

In the midst of the infernal din, Randolph's ear catches the music of a full brass band, which he is told is at Lee's headquarters, but whose sweet tones make him for a moment forget the terrible work of death in front.

But, "Look! look!!" says one, and with a fearful explosion, a cloud of white-looking smoke arises over the cemetery, "there goes a caisson!" In a different direction the same thing occurs; again a voice cries, "There goes another!" and still the carnival of death goes on. Poor horses! Poor dumb creatures! Subservient to the use and brutality of man, their destruction that day was fearful; in one instance alone, as many as eighty being killed in a battery of eighty-four.

At last the cannonading ceases as suddenly as it begun, and there came the climax of the war.

Acting under the orders of Lee, Longstreet gives the order to Pickett to charge, and with his brave Virginians, he places himself at their head, and jauntily as on dress parade he moves his men over the crest and descends the slope with the firmness, coolness and decision of a parade. The enemy in their astonishment stand transfixed, but for a moment, when admonished by a sense of self-preservation, every available Federal gun is trained upon his devoted band. Fire front, both flanks, plunging, and cross are no incentive to hasten or to unnerve those gallant heroes; but steadily closing up, they press forward with a determined, soldierly step, their faces beaming with hope.

Hundreds of crimson battle-flags fluttered in the breeze; the long lines of troops with bright arms flashing like mirrors in the sunlight were pressing forward toward the enemy.

Here was all the "pride and pomp and circumstance of glorious war," that has captured and fired the soul of man in all ages, and by its dread illusions turned his finer attributes into heartless cruelties, and made the grim horrors of this murderous art a merry-making allied only to those of devils incarnate.

Now, a point is reached where the rush is to be made; the lines are closed up and massed for the plunge. Here Kemper fell; then came the dash, and with it a clash of steel and crash of musketry in the very faces of the opposing sides. Now falls the gallant Garnett; and with the thrilling yell of the charging Confederates the flag of the Confederacy is planted upon the works of the enemy. Now it is that brave Armistead falls, severely wounded; and the wavering divisions supporting, becoming panic-stricken, broke to the rear.   Instantly the Federals poured their hosts upon Pickett, fairly enveloping him, and crushing him with the weight of numbers.

The Virginians make a brave effort with cold steel, but are met with a concentrated fire in front and on both flanks.   Still charging, never dismayed, under this fire they seem to melt away.   They have done all that men could do, and now the remnant returns, but with their faces to the foe, repulsed but not whipped. Slowly they returned, broken-hearted at their loss and failure, but covered with a halo of glory that will be with them forever.

The Federal pursuit was but a skirmish line, which fell back before a few discharges of grape and shell.

And thus the curtain dropped upon Gettysburg.   Night fell upon thousands of dead and dying, and the fate of the Confederacy was sealed forever.

Grim death reaped from the ranks of the alumni of the Virginia Military Institute a harvest, ripe in all the wealth of glorious record and fruitful example.

Upon this fatal field, and upon an area of almost insignificant size, lay the forms of five ex-cadets—Stuart, Patton, Jas. Allen, R. C. Allen,

Williams and Edmonds, all dead upon the field of battle, a mute attestation of their heroism and their devotion to their country and its cause.

The stars looked down upon the pale, upturned faces of many a loved form, and Randolph, with but a slight wound, came out of camp with a lantern, in search of a missing friend, accompanied by four privates, and passing through the now famous peach orchard, goes directly to the rock-riven slaughter pen of the Devil's Den, meeting with men of both armies engaged upon similar errands.

In the vain search for his friend his attention is attracted to the indistinct voices of men behind a huge bowlder, and stumbling over the stones and picking his way among the dead, he comes face to face with the ubiquitous Van Horton, holding in his arms the limp form of a man, whose feeble voice and long, white locks told of suffering old age. The flickering light of the lantern revealed a look of mutual recognition.

"It is an old friend," says Van Horton, "not fatally hurt, but painfully so."

Reminded of the gray locks at home, Randolph kneels by the side of the stricken man, and offers to his lips his own canteen. A draught and a sigh, and the unfortunate old man thanks him in the language and manner of a cultivated gentleman, and, earnestly scanning Randolph's face, requested his address.

Upon receiving it, with his gaze still riveted upon him, "What?" he says, "Phil Randolph of Virginia?"

More surprised than he, Randolph takes his extended right hand, and in mute astonishment listens to a revelation as painful as it was surprising.

"Blessings upon you," said the wounded man, "and now that I am in the hands of one whose name is a household one with me, please, Capt. Van Horton, secure my removal, or find Major Carday, who is near, that I may receive medical attention. I am safe with Capt. Randolph."

Van Horton is soon lost in the gloom, and the stranger, continuing, says: "I am the father of Sadie Carday, and came to the front oppressed with the fear of a mishap to my only son, and seeing the troops of Pickett falling back, I thought that pursuit would naturally follow; but I found our men in confusion, having suffered severely in the melee, when all at once your batteries opened to cover the retrograde movement, and a stray piece of shell struck me here," placing his hand just below his right knee.

"I like not this Van Horton," said Mr. Carday, "but he appeared just in the nick of time, skilfully bandaged my wound—no one paying any attention to me on account of my citizen's attire. What brought him here, I know not, being unattached, and, like myself, in citizen's clothing."

"A spy, I presume," replied Randolph, "as his forte lies in that direction; and that your estimate of the man is correct, allow me to say from my own knowledge that he is a scoundrel, and a robber in heart and in fact. But tell me, is any member of your family near you, besides your son?"

"None," he answered. "My daughter is now a guest of Miss Marguerite Darlington."

Thus patiently they awaited, until at last the sound of footsteps was borne to their ears, and a swinging light announced the looked-for assistance.

With rapid steps Major Carday approaches, and casually nodding to Randolph, laments his father's unnecessary exposure, and his unfortunate condition. Being introduced, he in a most cordial manner grasps Randolph's hand and with a cheery "Glad to meet you, Captain. Please give us a lift to the ambulance close by, and we will talk afterwards."

The old man being snugly stowed away, the Major turns to Randolph, and says:

"Now let me thank you; you are what Sadie says, 'the soul of honor,' and 'one of the best fellows on earth,'" and drawing himself up to his full height, fully six feet, with his bright face, dark hair and eyes, just the opposite of his sister, he appears as one who meant what he said and was happy to say it.

With thanks Randolph acknowledged the compliment, and tells him of his late interview with Van Horton; about his sister's loss, of the many noble traits of the heart and of the character, and of the gallantry, and last, of the love and devotion of poor Adjutant Mayne for the sweet sister now with Marguerite.

To all Major Carday listens with a sad and thoughtful brow; now turning his face he meets the gaze of Van Horton, and as quick as a flash of lightning the tell-tale frown of a furious hate mantles his face. Randolph notes the recognition now for the first time of the bearer of the wounded man's message. The Federal major, mindful of his obligation, with becoming courtesy, thanks Van Horton for his kindness to his father.

Van Horton, with the *sang froid* of an old campaigner remarks, "I am not insensible for the sufferings of my fellow-man, particularly of an old friend (sarcastically), whose courteous treatment under his own roof has so endeared him to my heart."

"This is neither the place nor time to renew an acquaintance not agreeable," says Major Carday, "and I beg to bid you good-night, Mr. Van Horton."

"Good-night," answers the wretch, now fairly aroused, backing from them and doffing his cap in mock humility. "I shall be pleased to carry for your friend any message of love or condolence, for I shall see your good people soon, Captain Randolph, whom I have no doubt await with anxiety my happy arrival—my sweet intended, Miss F——, so devotedly loves your brother and his pretty, little, pet sister."

Stung almost to madness, the Federal major lays his hand upon his pistol, but remembering the situation, calls loudly for the sergeant of the guard, the picket line being in close proximity, but before a search is well begun, Van Horton has disappeared in the darkness.

After exchanging many regrets concerning the phases of the war, the separation of friends, the conflict of brother against brother, the desolation of homes, and the ruthless destruction of life and property, and mutually expressing the desire of an early meeting under the shadow of the white wings of peace, each returns to his respective camp, and is soon lost in sleep.

Chapter VI.

'Twas midnight of the 4th day of July, 1864, when Randolph (who had lost his horse), seated in a captured Concord coach, which was loaded with delectable supplies, the fruits of the visit to Pennsylvania, was driven southward along the Seminary ridge in the direction of Fairfield, bound for Williamsport, Md. Here the pioneer troops were engaged, with the most primitive tools, in constructing the pontoons to cross the bulk of the Army of Northern Virginia. These boats were launched and floated down the Potomac to Falling Waters, a crossing but a few miles below Williamsport, where Lee crossed his trains, artillery and his troops in safety to the south bank.

Remaining late with Carter's Artillery, which held the bluff to defend the crossing, Randolph lost his tent, his supper and his reckoning in the dense cedars, and slept under the eves of a tent near by, suffering the miseries of a drenching rain, and the eternal drip, drip, drip of the tent till the dawn of day, when, to his disgust, the familiar voice of his own messmate told him that he had slept on the wrong side of his own tent.

The troops again took up their line of march, and their steady tramp soon brought them in sight of the gallant and long-suffering Town of Winchester; thence to Manassas Gap to "bag a Yankee brigade," which proved too big for the bag, as it turned out. The brigade consisted of two army corps, requiring a night tramp down by Front Royal, and a safe space of eight miles away by the brawling river to rest the weary and footsore men.

It was about four o'clock on the following day, when the division wheeled to the left of the road to go into camp, and Randolph was not yet dismounted, when an order was received for him to take the Pioneer corps to Thornton's Gap, a distance of some five miles, to bridge a stream at that place. That five miles added so unexpectedly to the march just finished, seemed to grow in length as the worn-out men straggled along.

But the point was duly reached, and orders were obeyed, but not before Randolph measured the depth of the quicksand with his horse, and gained an experience of navigating an animal on fence-rails from quicksand to *terra firma*.

The labor done, Randolph lost no time to gain access to the hospitable mansion of Mrs. Thornton, near by, and was welcomed by old friends and new, of both sexes.

The heart swells with the grateful remembrance of the good cheer, the cordial welcome of the sweet-faced matron, the good Old Virginia mother and grandmother, with a voice that cheered, and a smile that meant welcome, and a dignity and firmness with sweetness that was the stay of Jackson's grip upon the Valley and the bolster of the wearied soldiers' courage.

Oftimes memory has lingered over the recollections of that visit, bringing thoughts, laden with prayers and blessings, for the good Old Virginia matron who brought "home" to a soldier's heart, short though it was. Here Randolph encountered Colonel Morton Marye, who had left a leg upon the field of battle, and who was anxiously awaiting the arrival of General Ewell, who likewise had lost a leg.

The meeting of the two was of some importance, as Ewell's peg was too long and Marye's too short, and an exchange of pegs was in contemplation; and we are happy to add was consummated with mutual satisfaction.

It is needless to say that, though Randolph had an eminent regard for General Ewell, it was not supposed that inferior officers on duty were recreating in brick mansions, eating chicken, listening to the sweet tones of a piano, drawn out by the nimble fingers of a charming lady, and at the hour of retiring, to eschew tattoo and taps and luxuriate in a feather-bed. A sorrowful finale is to be recorded, and one indeed divested entirely of dignity, for the General, long expected, only put in an appearance in the we small hours of the night, and as he entered the front door our friend, Randolph, went out hastily at the back door. At that time the General could "cuss," and it was from a fear of extorting that sort of an effort which caused the irregular exit, although in later years that habit was but a recollection of the past.

After a tedious march, the division arrived at Orange Court House, and here Randolph received orders for detailed duty, and for fuller directions to report at Richmond.

A government is no government without red tape, and Randolph cared not how long they wound and unwound their tape, so long as his money held out; for quartered at the old Spotswood, he was happy in the company of old friends. There were present also many old ex-cadets of every official grade, all hob-nobbing and messing at the same table, and forgetful of all trials and dangers—past, present and future.

Donning his best suit, Randolph seeks No. — Franklin street, where a cousin of Marguerite lived when last he visited Richmond before the war. Remembering vividly, too, how he took the wrong direction homeward, and in the wee sma' hours anent the twal, was turned in the way of home and happiness from the precincts of Butchertown, by a kind and gentlemanly policeman.

Answering the door-bell, he was told that Miss Signor was at home, and was shown into the parlor, now carpetless; the carpeting doing duty now and for many days past as soldiers' blankets. Soon she entered, with the ease and grace which was a part of the woman. Gentle, pretty and intellectual, she was a model of grace, and of all the virtues that charm the heart, and exalt while they charm.

Advancing with extended hand, "You are welcome, sir," she said, "as all soldiers are who wear the gray. But tell me, whom have I the honor of addressing?"

Laughing, Randolph is in the act of answering, when she fairly screams: "Oh! Oh! you good-for-nothing scamp; you deserter, you fraud, you everything that is naughty, where have you been? What a great, long moustache you do sport, and it was but yesterday the beardless cadet, lost in revery of his true love, and gazing at the wrong star, lost his reckoning in the lighted streets of Richmond," and ceases only in a paroxysm of uncontrolled laughter.

Randolph meekly catches the contagion and joins heartily in enjoying the ludicrous picture.

"Now, Berta," pleads Randolph, "will you never learn to respect the tenderness of my poor heart? Think how I have suffered! Been up in Yankeedom, keeping the whole nation from visiting you and the seat of the Confederate government, and now you chaff me. Fie, for shame!"

"A truce it is," she answered; "but tell me, what did you bring from the raid?"

"First of all, my dear lady, these beautiful high-topped boots; a handsome and gallant cavalry officer had no further use for them in the place he was journeying to; a man of our Pioneer corps borrowed them, and being unable to get a No. 9 foot into a No. 7 boot, Secretary Trenholm's scrip made them mine."

"And is that all?" she asked.

"Oh, no," answered Randolph; "scores of wagons went into Pennsylvania loaded with hungry, footsore and barefooted men. Our wagons returned loaded with food for man and beast, and clothing, and our men shod to a man. As for our staff, we have flour, cut-loaf sugar, tea, coffee, apple butter, and, please don't faint! a whole barrel of whisky. Ah! your lips grow moist!"

"At least, not for the whisky," she answers,

"but men exposed, I suppose, must needs have it, and it must be so refreshing to the poor wounded; but I must say that our okra and sweet-potato coffee, when compared to the simon-pure, would be more apt to bring water to the eyes than to the lips."

Mindful of the object of his visit, Randolph says:

"Tell me of your sweet little coz, Marguerite. I will share my choicest rations with you if you will tell me 'heaps' of my little sweetheart."

"What a valiant lobbyman in the councils of Cupid!" says Berta. "You would bribe me; you judge me as Fannie P—— judged yourself when a cadet—'that the only way to reach your heart was by your mouth.' However, I have news, and good news. Would a surprise hurt you, or are you too well guarded?"

"Oh! no," answers Randolph; "Cupid flies, and the little fellow has a reckless way of flying his darts; videttes would be useless, and I am too old a soldier to be frightened. On with the surprise, and earn your bribe."

"Then, let me tell you," says Berta; "Marguerite is here in Richmond, and Sadie with her. Marguerite's brother Charlie is in the hospital, wounded in one of the many fights of the Stonewall brigade, and the girls are down with him now, with what delicacies we could rake and scrape together—some bought, some begged and some contributed, and the sum of all not much to brag of."

More than satisfied with the success of his visit, Randolph, in company with Berta, approached the hall door, when, as if by magic, the door flies open, and the ladies enter, Marguerite in advance. Berta quickly, in jest, introduces "Miss Darlington—Captain Price," and quick as thought Randolph puts his arms around the little lady, and says: "Yes, yours without price, my little one!"

"Oh, how you frightened me!" answers the willing captive, and the upturned lamp shows a lovely face, radiantly beautiful, with crimsoned cheeks and sparkling eyes, shaded by hair as black as midnight, and lips that to Randolph seemed to be lost in the luscious fragrance of their sweetness.

For a time questions of no importance to the reader are made and answered, with astonishing rapidity, till the hour of 12 calls for the lingering "Good-night!"

'Tis late and the city is wrapt in sleep, when Randolph reaches the Spotswood, where he meets his old fellow-cadet, Colonel Slaughter, of the —th Virginia, and together they find a banker, a boyhood friend, and together enjoy a supper "fit for the gods," the memory of which

is green and glorious of to-day; but whose mixt-
ure of every variety of stimulants, a vivid memory long remembering, involuntarily causes the
hand to feel the head for an aching recollection
of that joyous event.

Their stomachs were empty, their appetites
good, and delicacies never saw during the war;
the temptation was great, and though the Colonel badly limped from the effects of a bullet
through the thigh, they bore their burden like
men, and safely laid their forms, increased by
many pounds avoirdupois, upon their hotel
beds, and dreamed of feasting, and arousing
early in search of the nearest cut to the water
tank.

Breakfast next morning is hastily dispatched,
and Randolph looking "tired," but armed with
his promised bribe, is soon ushered into the parlor, and anxiously awaits the ladies.

As the group file in, Marguerite's quick glance
betokens the knowledge of a night of short
rest, but condones the offense, because has not
the offender just passed through the valley of
starvation and the shadow of death? Surely
one wagon train could not last always.

In this group now seated around Randolph,
happiness reigns supreme; quick wit and bright
repartee gladdens each heart, and shortens time,
that even the sombre dress and sad face of

Sadie cannot subdue, for in 1864 death was a
familiar event, and had knocked or was knock-
ing at the door of thousands of Virginia homes.

Belles, beaux, marriages, the war, the army,
the conduct of the officials, "Examiner" com-
ments, all were discussed, till a hush came from
the ringing of the front door-bell, and almost
immediately, two officers of the Artillery and
Engineer Corps, respectively, entered, and were
introduced as Captain Barton and Lieutenant
Rumford; when the ladies, almost in a chorus
in their eagerness to secure the aid of the new
arrivals in denouncing the remark which Randolph had let fall just before their arrival, that
he was in sympathy with the "Examiner," then
published in Richmond. Miss Berta claiming a
"court-marshal"; "charge, treason"; "speci-
fications, to be forthcoming."

Captain Barton claimed ignorance of the
whole matter, to which Miss Berta answers:

"Have you not seen Editor John M. Daniels' editorial saying, 'That if the Confederacy
fell, there should be inscribed upon its tomb-
stone, 'Died of a V,' ' referring to the angle
formed by Jeff Davis' Mississippi troops at
Buena Vista?"

"Captain Randolph hears the General Order,"
says Lieutenant Rumford, "let the court be
opened."

"Certainly," answers Randolph, "the court does not propose to deny me the right of thought, and of expression, and most assuredly I have committed no crime."

Quickly Marguerite speaks in defence of her lover, and says: "Perhaps fawning now may lead to preferment, and though silence is golden, it may lead to oppression or defeat, mayhap to both."

"Well and bravely spoken, my guardian angel," says Randolph, "and now let me divest your minds of one error, and recall to your minds a few facts of history."

"The assumption of the form of the letter V was not the outcome of the ingenuity of Colonel Davis, but simply the occupying with his lines the natural crest and conformation of the hill commanding the intervening valley. Furthermore, in looking over the field of our disasters, do you not perceive the direct origin of Daniels' ominous words? Look at Price, the idol of his army, beheaded at Richmond, and succeeded by Pemberton whom none knew, nor wanted. Behold the result! a retreat from Holly Springs to Vicksburg—locked up, and caught like a rat in a trap, not counting the bloody blunder of Big Black River. See again Joe Johnston wearing out the attacking army in detail by leading him away from his base of supplies, choosing his own ground, pounding him well, and cutting his communication off from his base of supplies; leaves him to repair damages, fix up and march again to receive the same dose. Yet, at Richmond, his head falls in the imperial basket, and a gallant officer not equal to the emergency, with the executive prediction, that he was one to 'strike a manly blow,' steps in, with a new programme, and with a campaign marked only by the carelessness or stupidity of allowing a whole army to pass near his sleeping troops, and with the bloody defeat of Franklin, nothing else is to be noted."

With flashing eyes he asks: "Do you see the terrible contrast with the 'manly blows' struck at Resaca, Kennesaw, Altoona, and upon every hill-top on the line of Johnston's retreat?"

A pause, and Randolph turns to Berta, and says: "I really think that I will have you put in the stocks, and to further punish you, when I get married, I shan't call you cousin."

"Wait, Captain," she answers, "till that time arrives; 'there is many a slip, etc., etc.' But let us drop such questions and talk of our own dear selves."

And now the usual chaff of young people, bent upon enjoying the brief moments of relief from camp, soon dissipates the hours, and the young men rise to leave, and Randolph last, for the words spoken to Marguerite are not many, but all of love and devotion—for the partings of those days were sometimes good-byes forever.

The three young men slowly sauntered towards the Capitol grounds, separating there for their respective hotels or quarters, and upon the arrival of Randolph at his room, he found a curt note scrawled upon a strip of paper:

" Waited here two hours to deliver orders; back at 6 a. m. to-morrow."   " ADAMS, *Orderly.*"

This ended his revery, and he retired; the old negro refrains which he had heard so often on the Mississippi steamers ringing in his ears, "Good-bye, my lover, good-bye."

Chapter VII.

Promptly Orderly Adams appears with his official missive, and saluting, retires to the sacred precincts of his bomb-proof post in —— department, and Randolph is left to read his orders. Being of a private nature and for the good of the service, and totally irrelevant to the issues herein, we simply state that the duty assigned was arduous, dangerous, and requiring nerve and good judgment to perform with safety and satisfaction.

Armed with an order to draw for a coadjutor, Randolph thought of none more worthy or acceptable than his former fellow - traveler, now Sergeant O'Rourke—and as future events showed, none better pleased to serve, or better able to fulfill the duties required.

Bidding an affectionate adieu to the angels on Franklin street, and draining a parting cup with his friend and companion of the memorable feast, Colonel S——, about 8 o'clock a. m., upon a lovely day, the two soldiers were seated on board the cars en route to their destination, via Lynchburg, and to a point some forty miles beyond.

Arriving late at night, our travelers disembark on the south side of the road, and, attracted by a glimmering light some distance away, proceed thither, guided, as it were, by this star of hope. In the days of his boyhood Randolph had been a guest at the hospitable mansion now sought, and whose venerable, though eccentric, host was his father's steadfast friend; but time had erased the map which memory should have retained, and they stumbled along as though perfect strangers in a strange land. Anchoring at the gate, and clinging thereto with the energy of wrecked mariners, superinduced rather by the expected appearance of some wicked and vicious quadruped of the genus canine, they venture a timorous "Hello!" which brings a watchful man-servant to the door, who bids them enter.

Here was the enjoyment of a blissful rest, and rising early, Randolph, standing upon the front porch, drinks in once again, and perhaps for the last time, the lovely scenery from as lovely a home as is found in any valley of Virginia. The house is situated upon the very crown of a gentle elevation, and is built of brick masonry, being one-story, with attic lighted with dormer windows; of a rambling style, but with large, airy rooms and a spacious hall, both front and rear, supplied with broad verandahs, whose columns were entwined with running vines and climbing roses.

In the yard, and to the right of the mansion, was the office, a two-room building, used when pressed. Between the two houses was a large granite block, about two feet deep, two feet wide and six feet long, having two basins chiselled therein, for the accommodation of those who desired to bathe their face and hands in the waters of a lovely spring hard by.

The host, a model farmer, as he was a model man, of massive build and sunny face, with long, flowing locks, now tinged with the frosts of more than seventy years, was nevertheless very democratic in his manner of dress.

Randolph gazed in silent admiration, and with thoughts of inexpressible happiness, at the beautiful landscape spread out before him. Once again he sees the familiar friend of his childhood, the Peaks of Otter, rising like a giant in strength and grandeur upon the right; the valley in front, with its varied verdure of corn, oats, tobacco, and its pasture of lowing kine and bleating sheep; and far beyond, in the distance, the long sweep of deep blue of the ridge of that name, bluer by contrast with the azure of the skies.

All this was much enjoyed, until his revery was abruptly broken by a friendly (if it was heavy) hand that fell upon his shoulder, and looking up, the kindly gaze of his old friend was met with the demand, "And where did you come from?"

The answer was easy, and with that easy grace which the old man, with even his osnaburg shirt and red bandana handkerchief swung around his neck, could not diminish. With such grace and welcome, he takes Randolph by the arm and leads him into the sitting-room, where a massive sideboard of mahogany is graced by elegant cut-glass decanters, all, need we say, well filled. Sugar, in meager quantity, was there, and on account of its rarity sparingly used. A glass of freshly gathered mint stood convenient for use.

Bidding his guest to partake, the good old man in an incessant strain talks of the war, his troubles, and of old times, until stopped by the draining cup; when by many coughs and much clearing of the throat, Randolph is made very positively and painfully aware of the fact that Sergeant O'Rourke is present and "not in it," but evidently desirous of joining in the libation.

The old Captain, for such he has been called for these many years, sees the object of commiseration, and, without further to do, cries, "Come, come, sir! and join us; we are only ahead; you are on time, and can catch up by adding to the quantity."

"I will, and thank ye," says the Sergeant,

and, evidently mindful of the words of his host, he fills his glass to the brim, and, bowing with becoming gravity, he swallowed the contents without drawing a breath, and wiping his mouth with the back of his hand, cleared his throat and said: "Bether than the stuff you were afther bringin' back from Carlisle barracks, Captain."

"You have drank some of the Captain's ten-year-old apple brandy, O'Rourke," answered Randolph.

"The saints be praised! The blessid apple brought trouble and misery enough to auld Adam, and busted up the family circle entirely, but sure Captain the juice of apples loike that would make a paradise anywhere without Adam in it. Sure I fale it in the botham of me brogans."

It is not long before the household are seated at breakfast, and to the almost utter demoralization of Randolph, a young Lieutenant S——, and an old ex-cadet, drops in, who is spending a sick leave, having enlisted in Mobile, Ala., while engaged in the noble and exalted position of sampling cotton in that port.

For the poor old devastated Virginia of that period, the table partook of a fascinating repast; and the event seemed to culminate in a meeting of friends, whose mutual records and reminiscences, when brightened and enlivened and brought back to memory, would make the old walls resound to the peals of joyous laughter. All of a sudden this was estopped by the disposition of our high-stepping and fancy lieutenant, actuated by the push and energy of those we fear as friends, and dread not as enemies. His desire was to speak, and none knew it better than poor Randolph, and none dreaded it more. Turning his adolescent figure to face our honest old host, he pertly says:

"Captain, how many bushels of wheat do you raise?"

Answer—"Five thousand."

Question—"How many of corn?"

"Eight thousand."

He asks of horses, cattle and sheep, and patiently the old man answers this catechism; whereupon this puerile ghost of a soldier, not knowing the ground whereon he treads, says in a spirit of advisement:

"'Cotton is King,' Captain; you should sell out and go south, and raise cotton, sir."

Never will I forget the look of mingled disgust and contempt which absolutely paled the old Captain's face (ordinarily red), as he turned upon the young man with the expression:

"D—n you and cotton, too! I wouldn't live out of sight of the Peaks of Otter for all the cotton states of the Southern Confederacy.

'Cotton!' 'Cotton!'" And with a sniff and a snort, he attacked his plate with renewed energy.

Needless to say, none enjoyed the rebuff more than Randolph, whose experience in the cotton region taught him the truth of the old man's words, and he felt that it was merited rebuke to the recreant fealty of a stupid Virginian.

It becomes necessary here to purchase horses if possible, and as the old Captain in his patriotic enthusiasm has disposed to the Confederate government all of his available stock, it was decided that Randolph and the old Captain should ride some six miles across the country westwardly, to secure the necessary mount, while O'Rourke should hold the office down during their absence; a servant also being sent to beat about among the immediate neighbors for horses, which, if sent, were to be examined and valued by Sergeant O'Rourke, now the supreme officer in command.

For at least an hour after Randolph's departure, our good Irish sergeant walked that yard, never passing the sitting-room door without thinking of the gladdening contents of the big glass decanters upon that mahogany sideboard. At last he rests before the door, holding his right elbow in the palm of his left hand, with his right gently carressing his much admired goatee, and concludes his reverie thus: "I'll do it, begorra!'' and walking in, he fills a tumbler to the brim and quaffs his spirits with the gusto of one who has the right, and of right enjoys it. Resuming his walk, his heart warms to himself and his fellow-man, and his legs beginning to tire, he hies him to to the office, which hardly affords him a chair before he is accosted by a plain, young, farmer lad, whom he invites to ''take a seat and sit down.''

In the absence of any chair, the lad promptly says, '' I ain't got any seat.''

''The Divil ye havn't!'' answers O'Rourke. Ye have a sate, and just put it on the steps.'' Now feeling, with the help of his libation, his importance as an inspector and purchaser of government horseflesh, he proceeds to catechise his visitor:

First, spitting high and far, and with an assumption of much grandeur, he asks: ''Phwat's yer name?''

''Isaac White, sir,'' the lad meekly answers. ''Was wounded, one of Jenkins' cavalry; father refugeed near here, from below Petersburg, and my pa sent me here to bring her up.''

''And sure, is she well put up, and will she stand the cavortin' of the boss?'' says O'Rourke.

''Of course she is, and of course she will; and moreover, she is as bright as a daisy,'' he answered.

"An' now ave yer plase," said Mr. O'Rourke, "an' how does she move?"

"Like a queen, and there is not her match in the country," answered the lad.

"She must be a honey, be jabers," said O'Rourke; "and sure it will take an ambulance to bring the Confiderit money to buy the queen. Now, tell me, is she quiet, gentle and well handled?"

"Oh, Lord bless you! yes; you jest see my ma and pa onst an' you'll be satisfied of that."

"An' how auld is she?" asked O'Rourke.

Isaac answered, "Just fifteen."

O'Rourke collapsed. "Howly Moses! trot her around, and let me auld eyes behold the queen of fifteen years that can bate the Captain's seven-year-auld, that he rode away from here this blessid morn. 'Arrah! go away wid ye! Phwat do yer take me fer, yer spalpeen?"

Upon which Mr. Isaac White rises in sheer stupefaction, not knowing whether the man was crazy or upon the road thereto.

But the climax was reached when he was invited, with proper flourish of arms and much dignity of demeanor, to walk in and take a "drop," and then hitch the queen to the rack till the Captain should arrive.

Whereupon the scales dropped from the eyes of Mr. White, and he proceeded to enlighten

Mr. O'Rourke that, at the request of his parent, he had accompanied his sister, of fifteen summers, to enter the employ of his host, and that she is now with the old man's good lady, and would not enjoy being hitched to the horse-rack.

"Ouch! Murther!" said the Sergeant.

"Kape, what I've said to ye to youre darling self, me lad; there comes no good to be afther prating around yer own sayerets; and moind ye, its bether by lots and gobs to be hitched to a rack, rather than a wrack, which often happens. Now will ye take a drop? That's a man as ye is. Now run, me honey, and give the dear girrul me love and dootiful regards intirely."

Which Mr. Isaac White, judging from his haste, is anxious to do.

Upon the arrival of the two Captains, some hours later, with two led horses, they find the gallant Sergeant slumbering hard and heavy, and seeking refreshment, soon discover the cause, when sounding the decanters.

A night of rest, a hearty "God bless you," from the host, and once more our travelers are upon the road, and for many days are engaged in carrying out the orders of ———— department, until caught in the advance of the troops of General John Morgan, composed entirely of cavalry, and which were moving in the direction of Greenville, East Tennessee.

With the sapient advice of Sergeant O'Rourke to "jine the cavalry" for a brief season, and favoring the idea with a hope of seeing the faces of the old folks at home, Randolph readily assents; and riding ahead of the command, they are *astonished beyond expression*, to find Morgan and staff ahead of them without escort, in a country if not hostile at least more than doubtful, and filled with Union sympathizers.

Randolph and his faithful attendant soon arrive, and is welcomed to the bosom of his parents, but it was accompanied with such a burden of fear and anxious expectation, that acting upon the information of his parents that, the Yankees were near the place in force, and that his capture or death was liable from reckless exposure, they waited until darkness had fallen, when mounting their horses, they quietly rode away to a safe hiding-place, near the village, and in easy view.

Early next morning our adventurers were aroused by the noise of beating hoofs upon the highway, and the rapid firing of carbines; the flying horseman which flashed by, and to the rear, being recognized as one attached to the body of General Morgan, quickly aroused the suspicion in the minds of the two experienced soldiers that this was the sequel of yesterday's recklessness.

D A—7

Remaining *en perdu*, Randolph argued that having accomplished their object, the Yankees would retire upon their main body. At night they returned to the village and learned the particulars of the death of Morgan.

Mrs. C. D. Williams, a most elegant, courteous and hospitable lady, and for many years a widow, was the magnate of the village; the possessor of a large, two-story brick mansion with basement, surrounded with ample grounds, having a well-kept garden of flowers and fruits, running down and extending to the main street of the village. At one corner of the garden, and fronting on this street, she had constructed a small church, dedicated to the use of the Protestant Episcopal denomination; in the diagonally opposite corner, and near the house, was the grape arbor, in which Morgan was killed.

The maudlin story of Morgan's betrayal by a woman of the name and family of his hostess, *has been a story of no foundation in fact.* It was, however, ravenously seized upon by "that woman," Miss F——, who saw another Randolph to punish, and another victim for her venom. And even in after years, periodically did this poor she-devil visit her imbecile rage, until at Atlanta, the poor brute who was paid to marry her and move away from home, put her where bad women trouble not, nor bear false witness against their neighbors.

It is an historical as well as an indisputable fact, that Randolph's father, and all the Williams family, besought General Morgan not to take the risk of stopping alone in this hospitable mansion, to which he paid no attention, believing it to be idle and inane fear prompting the advice. Strange to say, the one most innocent of all knowledge of the presence of the object of all this parade, and of the representatives of the parties herein mentioned, that this absent and unsuspecting member of a family above all reproach, should suffer from the poisoned breath of suspicion. Perhaps, the outcome of the vivid imagination of a frightened soldier, who left his General to be shot down like a dog, while he took safety in flight; or worse still, the relentless persecution of a vicious woman, debarred from her old associates, a social pariah, whose insane desire for revenge had deadened every sensibility of gentleness and virtue, which are the crowning glories of her sex.

The *absolute* truth of history is as follows, vouched for by Confederate officers who did not run away—men of truth and courage—backed by the knowledge of a member of the Confederate Congress, and attested by the Federal Commander, General Alvan C. Gillem, who com-

manded the Yankee forces that made the raid,
and in every way a truthful gentleman, as he was
a gallant soldier:

VICKSBURG, MISS., Feb. 13, 186-.

—— ESQ.—DEAR SIR: In answer to your letter inquiring as to the time when and from what person I had information of the whereabouts and movements of General
Morgan, on which my advance and the action of my forces
were predicated, and especially whether any member of
the family or household of Mrs. C. D. Williams, directly or
indirectly, conveyed to me any information on the subject,
I have no hesitation in answering. My command encamped
at Bull's Gap on the 31st of August, 1864. In the afternoon
of the 3d of September, Colonel J. K. Miller brought a boy,
some twelve years of age, to my tent. The youth informed
me that his name was Leidy, that he lived with his parents
in Greenville, eighteen miles from Bull's Gap; that at 12
m. that day Osman's Confederate scouts had entered
Greenville; that, fearing the loss of his mare, he had
sought to escape, but had been captured; that after remaining in Greenville till the arrival of Vaughan's brigade,
Osman's scouts had advanced with that brigade to Park's
Gap, where the brigade commanded by Bradford encamped; that the scouts then advanced in the direction of
my camp about a mile, and stopped at a farm-house for
dinner, when the boy escaped through a cornfield. These
soldiers and officers said that General Morgan would spend
the night in Greenville. Such was the intelligence of the
boy that I knew it was Morgan's purpose to attack me,
and I determined to take the initiative and attack him at
daylight. A brave, intelligent citizen guided us by the
Arnet Gap road, to the rear of the left of the enemy's position, the main body of my force advancing at 10 o'clock
at night by the direct road to Greenville. Colonel Ingerton
turned the enemy's left and getting into his rear, entered
Greenville without encountering a picket. Information

was obtained from a trustworthy woman that Clark's battalion and McClung's battery were on the further side of the village, and that Morgan and his staff were guests of Mrs. C. D. Williams. Receiving this information, Colonel Ingerton ordered Major Wilcox, with troops of the Thirteenth Tennessee cavalry, to charge into the village and secure Morgan. This order was executed with spirit and dash. Before Wilcox's command arrived at Mrs. Williams' house, its inmates were aroused by the firing in the streets and at the stables where General Morgan's orderlies, with his horses, were sleeping. The General and his staff, half-dressed, rushed out of the house and found the streets, on all sides, filled with National cavalry. In the *melee* and whilst attempting to escape through the garden, pistol in hand, and without being recognized, General Morgan was shot with a carbine, and instantly killed, by Sergeant A. J. Campbell, Thirteenth Tennessee cavalry, who was on horseback some eighty yards distant from Morgan, at the southwest corner of Mrs. Williams' lot. Sergeant Campbell did not know who the person was that had been shot by him, nor was the body recognized as that of General Morgan until the papers on his person were examined, nor will this appear strange when it is known that he was dressed in light blue pants, without cap or coat. It has been charged that General Morgan was shot after his surrender. The assertion is not only wholly groundless, but under the circumstances impossible. The soldier who fired the shot was at least eighty yards distant, and the wound clearly demonstrated that the ball entered below the right shoulder and came out near the left breast.

Such are the facts connected with General Morgan's death. Neither Mrs. Williams nor any member of her household gave me any information concerning the movements or position of the rebel troops upon which I predicated the movements of my command. It is very strange that such a rumor should have gained circulation, when a son of Mrs. C. D. Williams was present with General Mor-

gan and serving on his staff. It has been claimed that a
member of Mrs. Williams' household conveyed to me at
Bull's Gap information of the arrival of General Morgan in
Greenville. This report is utterly false. The only information received is set forth in this letter. About the time
Wilcox's brigade entered the village I attacked the enemy
in front vigorously, compelling Bradford's brigade to fall
back until it came upon Ingerton's command, when it
broke and fled in confusion. The news of Morgan's death
was rapidly spread by members of his escort, who escaped
from Greenville, which probably accounts for the rapid retreat of his center and right with scarcely an effort at
resistance. After the engagement, the body of General
Morgan was properly cared for by the captured members
of his staff, aided by my own staff. It was my intention to
send his remains to his friends at Lexington, Ky., but in
deference to suggestions of some of his staff the intention
was changed, and the remains were sent through our lines
under a flag of truce.

I am, sir, very respectfully, your obedient servant,

ALVAN C. GILLEM,
Brevet Major General, U. S. A.

And thus is one of the errors of the times discovered and corrected; one of those strange
falsehoods, born of malice, jealously or ignorance, and oftentimes used as an assassin's dag-
ger to stab in the dark or to murder the innocent. Under all circumstances Morgan paid the
penalty of his temerity, and the Confederacy
mourned the loss of a gallant champion.

Randolph, with his trusty sergeant, now turn
their horses' heads once again towards the camps
of General Lee, who hard pressed by the over-

whelming numbers of Grant, is falling back and concentrating upon Richmond and Petersburg.

Oppressed with anxiety for the loved ones at home, and fearing the continued efforts of the relentless Miss F——, whom now he believes will stop at nothing, he dismisses O'Rourke near the Natural Bridge, and hies him to the home of his lady-love for a brief sojourn.

Chapter VIII.

THE bright sun of a November morning shines down upon a body of men, clad, for the most part in the uniform blue of the United States army. A few negroes ride with them, seemingly, upon equal footing with the others. Each man has fastened some article of household goods to his person or his horse, and by the quick, jog-trot, the frequent turning of the head to peer over the shoulder, the anxiety of the rear files to keep well closed up, all gave evidence of a marauding crew, fearing pursuit, and seeking safety for their booty and their own worthless hides.

The commanding officer is none other than our ubiquitous Van Horton, who, drawing rein, checks his horse, until a sergeant—a slim, tow-headed mountaineer of some twenty-six summers of wild-cat distilling—draws near, and as they are now ascending a steep ascent of the mount-ain side, Van Horton addressed this Sergeant Lamb (and a blacker sheep never browsed upon the hillsides of East Tennessee) as follows:

" We have cleaned Cedar Valley this time, and with better luck. In the first raid Old Randolph did give us some trouble, and knocked over Sallie Jenkins. I always told her that men's clothes and grabbing too fast would be the death of her. I wonder if the pious old man won't get worried when he finds that he has shot a woman?"

"Not much!" answers the sergeant. "She had on pants, and the pants were blue, and that ended it; he and all his whelps, male and female, will rejoice."

"We got his old partner," says Van Horton, "the doctor, this time for sure. But, I say, Lamb, the old man was nearly gone the last time you strung him up!"

"Yes," says Lamb, with lamb-like simplicity; "he took lots of choking for a big, fat man, and an old man at that; but if I hadn't kept it up your saddle-bags would be lighter by a mite. When Major Tom Randolph finds raid No. 2 such a success, and his sweetheart's old daddy houseless and homeless, what shall we look for?"

"I have thought it all out, Lamb, while your mutton-head was resting in sleep. I have promised my precious stand-by, Miss F——, to remember the whole Randolph family. I have done up the old man and woman, as you know, for you helped me; we have turned Major Tom's little darling out of house and home; and when we have put our little captures in a safe place, we are going for the young man next. My goodness! how Miss F—— hates that young man!"

"It seems mighty funny, too," says Lamb, for I remember the time when she was mighty sweet on Tom Randolph. Both were 'stuck up,' away out of my company: but I noticed how she hung on to him—'twas Tommy this, Tommy that, Tommy to church, ball—and nothing unless Tommy was there!"

Laughing with the reckless abandon of a heartless ruffian, Van Horton, placing his hand familiarly upon Lamb's shoulder, and in a congratulatory strain, says:

"Lamb, on yesterday you gave the old doctor a dose, and an experience of one h——, but multiply that by four, and still that place is one of luxury in comparison to the hellish fury of a woman scorned, and she will spare neither the male nor female of the Major's name."

Having reached a place both shaded and well watered, and having put some thirty miles between themselves and their place of plunder, a halt is called, and the men are soon engaged in preparing for supper and a night's rest.

No pickets are out, for Van Horton knows well that all the Confederate cavalry are drawn in and massed near Morristown, for the whole force of Federal horsemen are moving on them, accompanied by a strong body of infantry, and if, by hovering near, and any mishap should occur to Major Tom Randolph, how easy it would be to turn it to his own account and carry the glad tidings to Miss F——, to receive her thanks and reap the reward of his prowess.

When all were sleeping, and midnight was passed, two silent forms arose almost simultaneously, and, with cat-like tread, took their way to the head of the gorge, where, beneath the jutting stone, whose moss-covered top was shaded by a huge old oak—a landmark of the region, they hid away the gold and jewels of the good old doctor so lately plundered.

Before the sun had risen these mountain thieves were in the saddle and traveling direct towards Morristown. Arriving shortly after mid-day near the village, and not knowing the situation of affairs, an ebony-hued contraband was directed to resume his dress as a field hand, and make his way on foot, to gather up all the information possible and return to the troop in their hiding.

In a country thinly settled and densely timbered, with few roads to direct the wayfarer, it was an easy matter to find a hiding-place, even for a brigade, who might look down with perfect security upon an army without a thought of detection.

Night had settled down, and the stars came out in the sky, shining brightly from their azure canopy; the crisp winds of November sighed among the dead and dying leaves, rattling in their dryness, and then falling from the bough which they had gladdened and decorated in the bright and happy sunshine of summer. The stillness of night is of that nature which brings to the mind sweet visions of love and peace, and to the heart a spirit of thankfulness for all the good gifts of heaven. No such effect is produced upon the motley crew lying wrapped in their blankets in this mountain valley.

The picket on duty is startled by a sudden burst of flame from a valley far away to the west: the heavens are brilliantly illumined for a few moments, then fade away. "Only another reb burned out," he thinks, when suddenly the cry of an owl. "hoo! hoo! hoo!" is heard. Knowing the signal, he answers, and soon the crashing of the leaves and twigs under the heavy tread of footsteps betokens the arrival of the expected contraband.

Having imparted his information, which is exhaustive, having visited both sides; the camp is soon wrapt in profound slumber—except one man, whose thoughts are busy of the morrow. Hate, jealously, love. if such as he could love, the hope of plunder, all passed in rapid succession through his heated brain, until nature, wearied at the strain came with a downy relief which soon lapsed into the hard breathing of a troubled sleep.

Morning finds the column of Van Horton in motion, and straggling in some semblance of military order they find themselves in front of Morristown and between the lines of the Federal and Confederate troops, and as the Federal cavalry were moving up to the attack, encouraged by the presence of overwhelming numbers, not from choice, but from an unfortunate necessity, our plundering crew were caught, as it were, between the devil and deep sea, and facing towards the village, prepared to join the attack.

As fate decreed, Major Randolph's battalion was posted just beyond the crest of the hill, the crest itself being occupied with a row of houses principally those of business; and being anxious for the fray, the Major had ridden into an empty shed-room, and, looking through an aperture, to his astonishment and infinite gratification, he sees before him the cowardly band of traitorous neighbors and the well-known person of their leader.

Riding back, he tells the glorious news, and his men, with quickened pulse, take firmer grasp upon carbine and sabre, and all feel that the day of reckoning is at hand.

The Federal cavalry cautiously approach, driving slowly the gray-clad skirmishers before them; when amid the booming of artillery and the crash of musketry, the bugles of the Confederates rang clear and thrilling upon the morning air, and with flashing sabres and rush of gallant steeds, they bear down upon the Federal advance. The shock causes a sudden recoil. when Major Randolph's battalion, galloping to the front, pour in a volley from their carbines at close quarters, which nearly annihilates the partisan band of Van Horton, and unhorses him under the very sabre of Randolph, who is spared his death or capture. for the son of our good old doctor so lately plundered, with a yell of fury, clove his unprotected head with one stroke of the sabre.

In the smoke and confusion, a fresh regiment of Federal cavalry came like a whirlwind upon the little band now fighting unequal odds, crushing and overwhelming them. Still Randolph cheered his men by voice and deed; to the command to surrender, he utters no reply; with a pistol in each hand, he fires away; when in admiration and magnanimous pity, an officer again demands a surrender. Alas! too late. Wounded already—with bowels torn, a sabre wielded with a strong arm, descends upon his shoulder, and Major Randolph falls, to be crushed under the iron-hoofs of charging squadrons.

One more hero gone to rest; one more home made sad and desolate, and one more heart to grieve of hope cheerished. now lost and gone forever.

The Confederates are beaten back, and a faithful soldier, neighbor and companion of Major Randolph. having never left his side, takes his mutilated body to a house near by. doing all that man could do to ease the last moments of his dying chief. With all his agony, no word of complaint comes from this gallant soldier. Now and then a frown of pain would distort a face always wreathed in pleasant smiles, a face at all times attractive—but now clad in the palor of death.

At midnight, when all was stillness. a movement of the wounded officer aroused the nodding Rogers, who, leaning over the quiet form, heard a gentle sigh. and then a murmur, in which the sweet word of "Mother" was spoken, and then all was still. The hunted spirit had gone, winging its flight where there are no more battles, and where the voice of the slanderer and calumniator is never heard.

An old "Knoxville Register." of November, 1864, lies spread out before me, yellow with age, and rumpled with folding and worn in creases.

With heavy heart and tearful eyes I read the following obituary:

"Major Thomas T. Randolph, —— Battalion, Tennessee Cavalry, Vaughan's Brigade, was mortally wounded near Morristown on the 15th. He was born in ——, Virginia, and was but 26 years of age, when he nobly yielded his life for the sacred cause of Southern independence.

"He entered at the commencement of the war, and was a faithful soldier to the close of his life. From June last until his battalion was transferred to East Tennessee, he was with General Early in the Valley of Virginia, and participated in all his hard-fought battles.

"His parents reside in G———.

"At the time he received his mortal wound he was in the advance, charging the enemy. With his last breath he expressed the willingness with which he submitted to the sacrifice of his life in defense of his oppressed country.

"Surely his noble patriotism will embalm his memory in the hearts of his countrymen, and the heroism of his death be a *lasting reproach to his detractors in life.*"

I lay the tattered memory away, and again resume my pen.

Chapter IX.

We will go back to a period of only a few short weeks previous to the events detailed in the last chapter.

It was at the close of a pleasant September day, for summer yet lingered in the lap of fall, and now the crimson rays of sunset were reflected with a softened splendor, in the cool, shimmering depths of the river, where it winds softly past the home of Marguerite, and so down to its junction with the historic old James.

Two people, in a gaily decked canoe, drifting quietly with the stream, felt the beauty and impressiveness of the hour. Need we tell the reader that the parties are Randolph and the fair Marguerite?

A long silence is broken by Randolph remarking, "I cannot believe that this is our last evening together; this week has been so like a dream —a very happy dream to me. I shall miss you so much when absent."

The maiden flushed faintly, but did not answer, and there was silence again between them, but in those dark and lustrous eyes there was a suggestion of unshed tears.

D A—8

They had reached the bank, and she had risen and turned her face so that he could not see it; he put out his hand to help her from the boat, and her's rested on it as he stepped on shore. Slowly ascending the bank, they crossed the main road running along the river, and made their way to the lovely cottage nestling upon the mountain side, the home of sweet Marguerite.

As they were passing an old trysting-place, a seat of woven twigs of hickory, Randolph, still holding the hand of Marguerite, drew her gently towards this place, seated her, and turning a gaze both ardent and sad, said: "And this, perhaps, may be our last and only meeting. We have loved so long, and I have fed my thoughts night and day with sweet memories of happy moments passed, and happier ones I hope to come. Marguerite, make not this the ending of all—let me this evening call you by the sacred name of wife?"

"No! no!" she answers. "I cannot marry you now; t'would break my heart to send you to the front alone, and I would be a burden in camp; a dutiful daughter, you know, makes a dutiful wife, and to obey my parents' command, prompted always by the love and welfare of their offspring, has always been the pride of my life and the safeguard of my happiness."

"Does he object to my being a soldier, or is it that my means are too limited?" asks Randolph in rather a sneering tone.

"Now you are cruel in your anger; it is neither"; and—and here she breaks down and hides her face and tears in her handkerchief, whereupon Randolph melts and pronounces himself an incorrigible stupid and a brute besides, and with an humble heart and contrite spirit he begs forgiveness, and is happy again to see the sweet face of her whom he loved so dearly smiling upon him in forgiveness of his ill-timed language.

"Father does say that you have made your home out West, and the people out there are so wild and desperate that he would not like to see me living in the midst of such a motley assemblage of such men and Indians—like a squaw in fact·"

At this timid and sapient revelation, Randolph is convulsed with laughter. The Marguerite of his vision, she of his heart, she of his very presence, "a squaw!" The idea is too ridiculous, and again he makes the welkin ring with peals of laughter; and feeling in the ecstacy of his mirth that a demonstration is necessary to establish his claim as frontiersman, he fairly scalps the maiden in his effort to kiss the cheek now crimson with blushes at the unseemly elation.

"Shall I go and see the Governor?" he asks.

"No, not yet," she answers. "I shall never give my love to any other but you. Go back to your command; love me always as you do now; let me hear from you often. Your country first, myself afterwards. Oh! if you knew my heart, you would feel the bliss of another life, free from war, absence, and the dread of danger. I will pray for you and—but here comes Sadie; do be cheerful and say nothing of the past.

Slowly approaches the sunny-haired little maiden, and reaching the lovers, she takes both hands of Randolph, and looking him steadily in the face, with melting eyes and lips that tremble with emotion, she says: "I have heard from home, and my father has so many kind words to say of you; he knew not that I should see you, but in his name I thank you so kindly for your good services in his behalf. What can I ever do to repay you?"

"Don't mention it, Sadie; glad to hear that the old gentleman got safely home; there is nothing which I would not do to make you happy."

"Oh, this war! Sufferings without number, anxieties, starvation and death!" says Sadie. After a pause she tells them "that tea is quite ready, and after partaking it I want to read to you the expression of my thoughts, so beautifully penned by 'Daisy,' a lady of Bristol, Tennessee.

In the meantime we'll adjourn to the parlor where Captain Randolph can read my father's letter, and you, Marguerite, can go and bathe those pretty black eyes. You've been crying."

"You are in error," says Randolph, very solemnly. "It is I who should show traces of recent tears. Marguerite insists upon my being a squaw-man."

"A what?"

"Why, a squaw-man; isn't that plain enough?" answers Randolph. "Wouldn't Marguerite grace a *tepee?* Think of her gorgeous trousseau of a bandana handkerchief and a red blanket! Let me disabuse you ladies of this Eastern idea, for beauty, elegance and refinement, the West, yes, the Far West, furnish parallel examples of excellence in knowledge and refinement, and frequently outvie their Eastern sisters."

Randolph's panegyric upon the West is here interrupted by the announcement that tea was served.

When the family are seated once more in the parlor, Sadie insists upon reading the poetry heretofore referred to as her thoughts and her prayer, and in a sweet, distinct voice read as follows:

"Implora pace, Oh, our Father!
　　Listen to us now,
　While in earnest supplication
　　Before thy throne we bow;
　Death rides forth amid the storm,
　　And war's red lightnings blaze,
　Dark clouds, and gloomy shadows fall,
　　And dim life's brightest days.

"The brow of Mars is wreathed in fame,
　　And the shining laurel bound
　With the hair of dead men, dyed in blood
　　From many a ghastly wound;
　The wail of childless parents
　　The insatiate monster claims,
　With shriek of helpless womanhood,
　　And the village home in flames.

"The ruthless shot, with hatred winged,
　　Swift rushing through the air,
　Tears the limbs of age and youth,
　　Nor spares the strong and fair;
　Homes once the scene of beauty's spell
　　Now desolate and drear;
　Where joy and plenty once did reign
　　Now woe and want appear.

"Life seems a dream—a horrid dream—
　　Of naught but care and pain,
　From which we'd give a world of wealth
　　To wake in peace again;
　Our land one scene of grief and sin,
　　A wrathful, rolling sea;
　Oh! Father, guide our nation's helm
　　From every danger free.

" Hush the storm-lashed billows--
　　Let us not longer grope,
　But give us o'er the darkened foam

The bright day-star of hope.
Hear us! Oh, our Maker! hear us!
  Turn the leaden cloud away,
And show us the soft 'silver lining,'
  That foretells the coming day.

" We would ask no selfish joy,
  Nor pleasure's boon implore,
But that the news of battle's woe
  Might wring our souls nomore.
Grant us Faith to bear us up
  Till death's dark hour is o'er.
Remove thy chastening rod, and give us
  Hearts to love Thee more.

" We have scorned the Shepherd's fold
  And wandered far away,
And cannot hope that we deserve
  The mercies that we pray.
Yet, spare us, Father, for the sake
  Of Him who died to save,
And rescue our dear Southern land
  From slavery's dismal grave.

" Oh, dry the eyes of those that weep
  For the loved ones gone;
Soothe children's cry, and woman's wail,
  And man's expiring groan;
Turn back the ruthless hireling foe,
  Let war's fierce tumult cease;
Stretch o'er us Thine almighty arm,
  Oh, God! we ask for peace!"

Thus finishing, she sadly says: "It looks hard for me to quote the 'ruthless, hireling foe,' when my good and noble brother is enlisted in the ranks of the invaders, and I a Yankee born;

but when I remember that all I loved was snatched from me by a bullet from the rifle of an imported foreigner, fighting for money, I feel half rebel.''

The host, from his easy chair, which his aged form holds down with 250 pounds of solid flesh and bone, his hands clasped before him and his thumbs revolving in concentric circles, thus breaks the pause:

''I admire your verses, Sadie, as I admire you; they breathe a sweet perfume of peace and piety. Since Jackson's death, our old neighbor and friend, I have thought more about a peaceful solution of all our troubles; with his life went all my hopes of freedom and success.''

'' Let us not bring camp-talk to this charming circle,'' says Randolph; ''we are surfeited elsewhere. I will gladly volunteer to escort Miss Marguerite to the piano to cheer our hearts with sweet song.''

The music which once won the heart in college-boy days again lingers in the ear and thrills the soul with memories of happy moments in days long past; the hours fly swiftly by, and late the ''Good-night'' is spoken, and stillness reigns in '' Rose Cottage.''

Early next morning Randolph arose, and, wandering aimlessly among the shrubbery, he espied a moving object coming down the river road. It proved to be a man, and nearer still it proved to be a soldier, equipped with knapsack and blanket.

To the question of "What command?" the soldier halted, and gracefully saluting, answered: "Company K., 1st Regiment of —— Troops, and that being lately transferred, was on his way to report to Captain Randolph at Petersburg."

"But Captain Randolph is a member of the staff of General R——, and I am the Randolph, and will leave in a few hours for my post."

"The stranger answered that "Captain Randolph is no longer on his staff; your General was killed in the Valley; he died like a soldier, with his feet in the stirrups and in front of battle."

The gallant hero dead! The friend of his boyhood, and of his manhood, gone forever from his gaze. His eyes grew moist, and the helpless spirit of the inner man cried out in agony, "Thy will be done!"

Bidding the soldier to await their breakfast, the solemn meal is soon dispatched, and but few hours elapse before they are steaming to Petersburg and its grim trenches, bidding defiance to Grant and his hosts.

CHAPTER X.

FATE, with some, and the "decree of an all-wise Providence" of another, has been the ready method of thousands in solving the cause or effect of a momentous occurrence in man's life; but to the hard thinker and the more material mind there seems to be "a missing link" in the solution of the extraordinary facilities afforded the viciously wicked of evading death, and oftener of securing a fortunate and happy deliverance from impending danger.

It is an adage that "the good die early," but a great many die early, and it does not follow that all that die early are good; and perhaps the bad ones who linger along are given more time for redemption by a kind Providence. Let us hope so, for it seems that neither Fate nor Providence had decreed that Van Horton should die on that bloody hillside at Morristown. And we shall proceed to follow this worthy, after his fall, when his troop was routed by Major Randolph's battalion.

Badly hurt and faintly breathing, he was carefully moved to one of the houses of the village, and after weeks of wavering between life and death, he was at last able to be transferred, and was accordingly forwarded by train to Washington, D. C. Emerging from the hospital a shadow of his former self, his forlorn appearance assisted by his artful skill in deception, enabled this Union officer to parade his wounds and his person for the admiring gaze of the social circles of Washington.

With the good living and charming festivities of Washington, Van Horton was soon himself again, and as the winter was fast drawing to a close, his thoughts naturally turned towards the reorganization of his band, and the means of replacing those who were left on the hillside at Morristown.

While quietly seated in his apartment, his war-like schemes are suddenly dissipated by a timid knock at the door, and in answer to the invitation to enter, a messenger appears and hands Van Horton a daintily perfumed note, which proved to be an invitation to attend an entertainment at the residence of Mr. Courtnay. There were to be tableaux vivant, music and dancing.

Knowing Mr. Courtnay to be among the wealthiest of the wealthy, one of the largest army contractors and a power at the throne, an acceptance was written immediately.

The hours went by with wearisome step, but

the moment came at last, and alighting from his
carriage, his person arrayed in the gorgeous uniform of a colonel of cavalry, he steps upon the
Brussels carpet, laid down from the curb across
the broad sidewalk, and enters the brilliantly
lighted parlors of the lately-fledged monetary
lordling, where his eyes are dazzled at the flash
of many lights, the lovely hues of silks and
satins, the beautiful array of ferns, flowers and
plants, while decorating rest the wearied eyes
with their soft, deep green; while the ears are
assailed with the chatter of men and women,
varied with the merry laugh of some happy
maiden, or with the inharmonious haw! haw!
haw! of the opposite sex, but all chastened and
subdued by a splendid orchestra, who sit in
improvised orchestral seats before a large curtain.

After a formal introduction, Van Horton lays
siege to the eldest Miss Courtnay, whose stately
figure, bright gray eyes, and light-blonde hair,
has had the effect of adding a percentage to the
value of her inheritance in the eyes of her gallant escort and new-born admirer.

Turning to his companion, Van Horton says:
" Fresh from the scenes of bloodshed, and the
tameness and manifold sorrows of the hospital,
what a glorious feast for the eyes and for (im-
pressively) the heart," and looking tenderly

down into the eyes of the lovely woman by his
side, he adds: "For one so humble as myself,
without prestige or record, I might say that it
all far exceeds my deserts."

"Your deserts!" she echoes. "Colonel Van
Horton, how can you say such things? Is it to
your modesty, or are you not endeavoring to
presume upon the ignorance of your company?
Can I not read? Have I not ears to hear? Ah!
The vanity of man."

Pardon me the suspicion of ignorance," he
answers, "and least of all any doubt of the
power of your eyes, and I thank you for your
kindness in imputing to my modesty that which
might have been more properly set down to my
ignorance."

With a face beaming with animation, she says:
"Do you pretend to say that you are ignorant of
the fact that you have been promoted to the
rank of colonel, and that your gallantry has
been mentioned by *special order?*"

"Ah!" he answers, " it is all the mere routine
of a soldier's life," and showing an unconcerned
air for the honors heaped upon him, which he
calculates will impress his companion with the
nobleness of his soul, which seeks only the glory
and maintenance of "the flag," he leads her to
a seat where the tableaux can best be seen, as
all are now being seated, attracted by the an-

nouncement, followed by a grand overture by
the orchestra. The curtain rises on

Scene 1. "*Deserted.*" A grief-stricken
mother kneels by the bedside of a sick child:
with disheveled hair and eyes uplifted, she im-
plores Heaven's help for a worse than widowed
woman, and for the safety of her suffering child.
A little boy with golden ringlets falling upon
his shoulders, stands near, gently fondling his
mother's hair, while the scattered ornaments of
the room show a confusion born of misfortune
and pent-up sorrow. The outside scenery is of
an English cottage home, nestling in a wealth
of shrubs and flowers and creeping vines; its
trim walk, its diamond-glazed windows and
wealth of colors, contrasting so dismally with
the interior. But not on this was Van Horton's
eyes riveted, but upon a little sign-board which
read:

"TO MELROSE ONE MILE."

Van Horton looks with bated breath and
startled interest, when the soft voice beside him
remarks: "Lovely, isn't it? My cousin volunteered her services and promised this a success;
I am so pleased that you are interested."

"Indeed I am interested," he answers, and
with a voice strangely altered, he asks: "And
to what has this scene a reference—a mere fancy
of the brain, I presume?"

"I can only refer you to my Cousin Sadie; she is the author and originator of all; she is a great favorite of my father."

"Ah! really," he replies, and silence follows, until is loudly announced:

SCENE 2. "*False in Love and False in War.*" To the left of the stage and right of the audience was a man, an almost *fac-simile* in size, age and appearance of Van Horton, kneeling in the attitude of a lover pleading his suit, while bending over him in all the glory of a triumphant coquette, stands no less a person than Miss F——, of doubtful fame; old men and women and young girls kneel with uplifted hands holding jewels and money as offerings, while young children cower in fear behind them—with slow music the curtain falls.

"Your cousin has a genius for the lugubrious," says Van Horton. "Is this the end?"

"Oh, no; only one more scene," says she. Why do you not applaud with the rest? I am sure it is beautiful, and Sadie has worked so hard."

He evades an answer by asking: "And who pray, did you say was the gifted author of our tableaux?"

"It is my cousin, Sadie Carday. Why she is just lovely; so meek and gentle, and besides she is just out of the rebel lines, but her gallant

and loyal brother is the treasure under our roof,
and condones all of Sadie's rebel proclivities."

Van Horton feels the sand giving away beneath his feet, First, Sadie Carday here, whose
very tableaux were studied events of his life;
and now her brother appears upon the scene,
who is spoken of in the language of pride and
affection and so studiously expressed, thus leaving him hopeless and helpless in his artful and
wicked designs. And Miss F——, when and
how came she here? This, and much more
flashed through the wondering brain of the
treacherous Van Horton.

Oh, man! wait and see! Heartless and brooding crime begets a multitude of woes, that all the
efforts of wealth and intellect cannot still, and
seldom assuage.

"I will introduce you after the next piece,"
says Miss Courtnay, "and I flatter myself that
you will surely fall in love," and immediately
the tinkle of the bell is heard, and there is announced:

SCENE 3. *The Fruits of Slander and Woman's
Hate.* The lights are burning dimly; a dark
shadow falls upon the scene; slow, dirge-like
music falls faintly upon the ear. An aged man
and woman are bending in mute despair over all
that is left of their noble soldier boy, while a
beautiful woman, with her long, golden tresses

falling over her shoulders kneels in prayerful attitude at his feet. The background is a well-executed scene of a wrecked and ruined home.

The make-up of the figures are of Sadie's creation, and are known to herself, and more especially to one other, and that "one other" is Van Horton, who, with all the callowness of his robber-heart, has suffered an agony of mingled wrath and hate. Well does he know that Washington is no place for him; but, first, he must know what brought Sadie here, and, with that end in view, he casually remarks to Miss Courtnay:

"And does your cousin reside here, or is she only visiting?"

To which she replies: "Only a visitor, as her brother, who, by hardship and exposure, is now confined to his room in this house, needs the attention of so sweet and skilful a nurse."

And now the curtain falls, the representations are ended, and the guests are rising from their seats and scattering over the spacious rooms in quest of friends and enjoyment. All seems confusion, and happily for Van Horton, he finds a suitable occasion to accomplish his end.

Suddenly he remembers "that urgent business, official of course, demands his attention at this very hour (looking at his watch); except for the appointment previously made, he could not find it possible to tear himself away, but duty, imperative duty alone, could cause him to deny himself the happiness of his present company, with whom he had so much enjoyed the delightful representations which had just been given."

And with much more of the same stuff, before Sadie could put in an appearance, our gallant, newly fledged colonel has dropped a crisp shinplaster into the ready hand of the obsequious porter, who politely hands him his chappeau and helps him into his ample overcoat.

Seated in his carriage as it whirls him to his quarters, his thoughts are troublesome ones, and he asks himself over and over again: "How came these things known to Sadie—by letter or in person?"

Verily, the way of the transgressor is hard.

When Sadie enters she is overwhelmed with congratulations, but when meeting with her cousin there is a mystic recognition, that indescribable look—part surprise, part contempt, and another greater part of "there, didn't I tell you so," which only a woman can express without lip or tongue.

Then bursting into laughter, Miss Courtnay relates the conversation of the doughty Colonel —his ignorance of Miss Sadie, his enjoyment of the scenes, and his sudden call to duty.

To all of which Sadie listens with the greatest attention, and remarks:

"We have squelched the hateful imposter, and my Southern friend, Marguerite, will have an interesting, as well as instructive, budget of news to impart in her next letter to her intended. I am so glad that I posted you so well as to the character of the man. You must have played your part admirably."

"What a strange coincidence that you should be thrown into the society of this man's deserted wife!" says Miss Courtnay.

"Not at all," answers Sadie; "there are thousands making inquiries at the bureau at which my father presides, and when this particular inquiry was made 'Van Horton' was the middle name used and not the surname, and getting from the lady his description, I placed him in a moment. My greatest wonder is how such a nice woman could cross the ocean for such a trifling fellow."

"Let the man go," says Miss Courtnay, "and let us enjoy the ball."

"I wish the ball was over," says Sadie, with an air of fatigue. "I shall not dance; but, mark my words, 'imperative duty'" (Sadie says this with marked emphasis) "will cause Colonel Van Horton to leave Washington before the flag rises over the dome of the capitol tomorrow."

And leaving their cosey corner, they mingle with the happy throng.

And true to Sadie's prediction, before 12 o'clock next day the Colonel is steaming towards Sherman's army marching on to Atlanta.

Chapter XI.

NEVER before in the history of nations is there presented a spectacle of such pure and unfaltering devotion, such grandeur of courageous suffering, and such sublimity of sacrifice as was presented by the citizens and troops defending the gallant old Cockade City of Petersburg, Virginia.

With four millions of negroes behind them, encouraged by every art and appliance of a cunning and relentless foe to deeds of violence, of arson, plunder and murder; with the ships of a nation a century old blockading their ports and harrying their coast, a new-born Confederacy, of itself and by itself, struggles for life and liberty.

The unequal struggle still goes on. The winter of '64-65 is a hard one for the Army of Northern Virginia, poorly fed and poorly clad as they were; still there is no lack of faith in the success of their cause, nor thought of surrender. If a thousand Yankees are slaughtered, two—yes, five thousand more are ready to supply their places from the criminals and slums of Europe: but if one hundred Confederates are lost, who are to fill their places? Nearly true was the Yankee General's remark. that "They had robbed the cradle and the grave."

The bulk of the Confederate army is occupying the City of Petersburg and vicinity. Grand, old Petersburg! Her gardens now are torn with shot and shell. her houses razed and crumbling under the incessant fire of the enemy, her helpless and infirm exposed to all the hardships of war's most fearful trials, and, added to all, is the gaunt figure of want, which stalks in their midst with threatening mien, and the grim monster, Death, reaps with both hands from war and famine.

The lines confront one another, extending from the Weldon railroad, on the right, around the city, and following the line of the Richmond & Petersburg railroad and east of it, to and about the City of Richmond.

The works of both armies are upon an extensive scale, and seem almost endless when viewed from a single point. Well-equipped batteries peer out from their embrasures in forts, redoubts and salients, connected with trenches and parapets, affording protection to the troops laying behind them.

Now and then a solitary bastion fort of the Yankees stands out in an isolated position, mounting its heavy siege guns and flying its big garrison flag—a mighty hedging machine—to accomplish by numbers and hunger what cannot be done by feat of arms.

Randolph has been here now many weeks, and, early one morning, as he emerges from an addit some twelve hundred feet long, to whose mine, at the end of it, the Yankees were offered many inducements to approach, he unexpectedly and most gladly meets an old fellow-cadet, General Lane, who now with his infantry brigade supports the big guns of Battery 45, served by a detachment of the glorious old Washington Artillery, and enjoys some moments of conversation and happy reminiscence.

Having met this command before, Randolph notes the appearance of their ranks, thinned to a skeleton by battle, sickness and hard service, and leaves for his camp in a saddened frame of mind

Tired, hungry and low-spirited, he sits wearily down in his tent to await the call of "grub." Suddenly his ears are saluted by a cheerful call of "Mail! Mail here!" and, listening, he hears called aloud, "Captain George P. Randolph!" accompanied by the remark, "and from a woman, too, by jingo! Look at the fist!"

Very soon the letter is before his gaze, but shuts out all thoughts of hunger and weariness, and adds to the weight of his troubles a load as heavy and burdensome as it was unexpected.

In brief, it tells him of the burning of the home of Marguerite, of the loss of all the valuable improvements attached to the place—all given to the flames by the barn-burning raid of Hunter—and also tells of their intended removal to Columbia, South Carolina, as a point of safety; for was it not there that the Confederacy printed their money? and with expressions of devotion, closes with a prayer for his safe delivery from all danger by sickness and battle.

His hunger appeased, his weariness of mind tempts him to wander among his fellow-officers, when even this privilege is denied, for an orderly curtly tells him that his presence is demanded immediately at headquarters.

Upon reporting, he is ordered to take two days' rations and twenty men and report to General G——, near Rives Salient, at 9 o'clock p. m.

Promptly he has crossed the pontoons and is wending his way through the old "Cockade City," a title earned in 1812 and glorified in 1864.

The moon, in queenly garb, was flooding all nature with brilliant, silvery light; the house-tops glistened with the frosts of the chilly night, and the deep shadows of tall houses, dark and tenantless, are checkered with the flickering lights of those who cannot or will not leave.

The streets are deserted, ploughed with shot and shell; the fine houses on Bolingbrook street a continuous line of wreck and ruin, with falling walls and tottering chimneys; now and then the sullen roar of heavy guns is heard, but the sharp report of the picket's rifle is never-ceasing.

. Every step unfolds a vision of the incarnate deviltry of grim-visaged war. Bomb-proofs upon private grounds, for the security of the owners in case of bombardment, are numerous; everywhere bears the evidence of long months of unceasing struggle.

Randolph reports for duty, and is assigned to the charge of a work of pick-and-shovel, for which he prepares to rest in the folds of his blanket, while waiting the "dark of the moon."

It is past midnight, when the picket gently places his hand upon his shoulder and tells him "it is time."

Arousing quickly, Randolph has his men in hand, and with string and pegs, they mark the line, and burrow like so many moles, until the coming of day. when the unsuspecting eyes of the enemy behold debatable ground no longer, but safely behind the fresh-raised earth are good men, with rifle and bayonet, to hold it.

As an evidence that this approach to a closer relationship than is recognized as agreeable, from right and left and front a storm of shot and shell are poured upon them, but lying down close. hugging the ditches, they spend a "long, long, weary day," listening and watching.

Night falls again; a comparative stillness follows, and at the same time as before they begin to extend the work, but not as before, unopposed or unseen. for in a twinkling sheets of fire flash from the parapets of the enemy, while their artillery opens with a roar that shakes the earth, killing and wounding several and driving the remainder to the cover of their pits.

This brought on an interchange of compliments between the opposing batteries, and for two long hours the din was incessant, the flashing guns and bursting shells making a pyrotechnical display wondrously terrible but fascinating to the gaze.

As the men lay closely hugging the inside of the ditch while all this grand display was going on over their heads, no one had noticed the stillness of Randolph as he lay upon the ground, but his nearest file thought that by the peculiar position of his arms and body that it was not natural for one uninjured, and shaking him, he . got no response; then it is found that he is badly wounded and insensible.

The two hours of steady firing gradually tapers off to a single gun away down by Pocahontas Bridge (or where it was), and finally it, too, ceases, and only the " pop! pop! " and never-ending night picket firing is heard.

At that darkest hour, just before dawn, four men carrying the litter on which lies now our wounded Captain, are hurrying with noiseless steps by the very route by which they had tramped so hopefully but a few hours before.

Upon examination it is discovered that the wounds, while painful, are not of a serious nature, and after the patient and skilful services of the regimental surgeon, our hero is left to his nurse and gentle slumber.

Soon in a condition to be moved, Randolph remembers the abiding place of Marguerite, and who could better play the part of physician and nurse than she? And would not the Confederacy have one less mouth to fill? Such pleading with the gentle and kind-hearted surgeon secured for Randolph a pass and transportation to Columbia, South Carolina.

In the latter days of the Confederacy, in those days of wheezy, overworked engines and rickety cars, who could portray the discomfort, the filth and terrible trials of a wounded man, jostled, side-tracked; in one hour hot, the next freezing cold; wretched, starved, and burning with fever and thirst?

The memory of that trip clings like a nightmare, and whose recollection is brightened only by one incident. Falling into a doze, and upon opening his eyes at some point between Danville and Charlotte, Randolph was surprised to see the sweet face of an elderly lady bending over him, smiling with a cheerfulness refreshing to a man in his depressed state of mind and body.

"You have been sleeping," says she; "I hope that it has been a refreshing sleep.

Buoyed by the look, the voice, and the good old face peering out of the curtains of one of those old-fashioned "sun-bonnets," sacred in the memory of our childhood days, he answers: "Yes, I feel much better, but I cannot understand why our engineer wants to jerk the life out of us, or break his couplings, every time that he starts to move."

With the same sweet, winning smile, she answers: "You are speaking from the effects of the jerks upon an empty stomach, and as I have a basket expressly for sick and wounded Confederate soldiers, I make it my daily business to travel up and down this road, a volunteer, for the special service of finding such as you."

And suiting the action to her speech, she beckons her waiter and regales our hero with viands to which he has long been a stranger, and which in long years after he gratefully remembers.

Perhaps this will recall to many a grateful

heart that good old lady, the ministering angel
of comfort, whose kind words and gentle touch
had soothed so many suffering soldiers, and
whose well-filled basket brought cheer and happiness to many a wan and hungry Confederate.

Changing cars at Branchville, South Carolina,
but a few hours' run brought him safely to
Columbia, where our hero is met by the blushing and happy Marguerite, who waves on high
in exultation the Chief Surgeon's permit to
quarter him at the home of her he loved so well.

Chapter XII.

FROM Petersburg to Columbia—Oh! what a contrast! At the one, strife and bloodshed, the rattle of small arms and the thunder of the big guns; pale want and grim desolation stares all with the grimace of an insatiate demon. At the other is music and the dance; gaily attired ladies and well dressed gentlemen, sprinkled but too frequently with gold-laced officers, parade the streets.

Worn with fatigue, and still suffering from his wounds. Randolph retires early, but not to sleep; thoughts come and go like lighting-flashes through his fevered mind. The transition has been too sudden, and all seems too unreal. Now, forgetful of his situation he listens for the incessant picket firing; but no, there is the sweet voice of some fair daughter of Carolina trilling the plaintive melody of Il Trovatore. "Ah, I've sighed to rest me."

Randolph thinks, too, of the gallant few of over-worked, ill-fed and long-suffering soldiers, who uncomplainingly shiver in their trenches— dying, and ready to die in defending their work.

Wearied nature at last asserts her rights, and

he sleeps that sleep which comes with change of place and new surroundings, deep, but full of the grotesque imagery of a disordered mind. While dreaming that he was leading a train of cars to capture Marguerite, who was being taken away by the Yankees, he was unhorsed by a woman with a basket, who, with her threatening carving-knife awakened him with a sudden start, to find that he had slept till 9 o'clock a. m., and that the sun was brightly shining outside of the drawn curtains.

There was no disposition to arise, but rather the reverse, and with a dull pain in every joint and each wound, a racking headache, he rather wished for the early arrival of some Good Samaritan.

Not long does he wait, for a gentle knock is quickly answered by the expected "Come," and a servant enters, who is directed to call for medical aid. This has the effect of bringing the host and hostess, the parents of Marguerite, quickly to his bedside, who, in a short time, are followed by Surgeon Fisher, who, with the deliberation of one who has seen service in the field, looks at the patient, smilingly asks how he feels, remarks on the pretty morning, and is all the time removing his overcoat, and then is —mum.

With tender and skilful hands the wounds

are unbandaged, and then it is discovered that much has gone wrong during the three days of inattention during travel.

Suffice it to say that with the severity of the operation, the depleted state of the body of the patient, and the high and almost ungovernable fever which held him in its fast embrace, the good old surgeon had a hard fight, and the patient a close shave for life.

On the seventh day Randolph opens his eyes upon a scene never to be forgotten. Sitting close to his bedside was Marguerite, her elbow resting upon a chair, holding her cheek in the palm of her hand, fast asleep. Her face was turned to him; evidently she had fallen asleep while intently watching him. What a wealth of happiness to him to gaze, and to watch unmolested that face he loved so well. He could almost feel her breath upon his cheek; still she slept and still he gazed; and, as if warned by some subtle agency, she opened her eyes to meet his own, exchanging a look of happy surprise.

" Well, sweetheart, I have watched over you while you slept, have proved myself a true sentinel, and now won't you reward me for my services with just one sweet kiss?" Thus speaks the sick man.

Without any shrinking prudery, she answers: " Indeed I will, my brave knight," and kissing him, and again for good luck, she pauses to ask: "Do you not feel much better, dear?"

He answers: "Ever so much better; I feel like a new man—wonderfully refreshed; rest of body and mind was what I wanted. Tell me, darling, how long have I slept?"

"Never mind about your time of sleeping," says Marguerite. "Keep quiet now, like a good boy, while I go and send the glad tidings to Doctor Fisher," who soon arrives and makes all happy by announcing all bad symptoms passed and predicting a rapid convalescence.

At the end of three weeks Marguerite prevails upon the good old folks to invite company to meet the Captain, their guest, at their house, which is granted with some gruntings, provisos and much ominous shakings of the head at the possibility of supplying the comforts for the inner man.

Marguerite answers, that they "would make it up by giving them a taste of Old Virginia hospitality, and as most of the people were South Carolinians, that they would be content with rice."

The eventful evening came at last, and with it to the hospitable mansion of Captain D——, the *elite* of Columbia. Beauty, grace and elegance of manner made up for the lack of gorgeous costumes, and wit, music and the dance

D A—10

went merrily on until the wee small hours anent the twal.

But not entirely recovered from his hard wrestle for recovery, Randolph, with Marguerite leaning upon his arm, saunters into the sanctum sanctorum of the Pater, who calls it his study, where his most studious efforts are directed in the extraction of as much enjoyment as possible from a fine old meerschaum, now grown a beautiful thing of colors. Thither also, the older members of the throng masculine had come for a friendly chat and a smoke.

Upon entering, a venerable gentleman arose, and with the courtesy of the chivalrous of bygone days, politely asks if smoking is offensive.

Marguerite answers, "Not at all; do continue smoking. I am accustomed to the smoke of tobacco, good tobacco, at least, and my father is too good a judge to offer you anything bad."

Continuing, the old gentleman, who proved to be an attorney and resident of the City of Charleston, says: "I am delighted to have the pleasure of your company Miss Marguerite, and quite as much so to see Captain Randolph, to whom I extend my hearty congratulations for his safe delivery from all his trials."

Randolph gracefully acknowledges the compliment, and adds that he will soon be able to

return to his command; that Lee can spare not
a man; or, "mayhap, I may be needed here, as
Sherman is turned loose without opposition."

A Colonel Stout, of militia fame, remarks:
"I notice that the march to Atlanta by Sherman is *un fait accompli*, and now that Hood is
away up north, may not this man with his immense army take it into his head to march east
and then northwardly, and lay waste the
country?"

This suggestion or question creates a diversity
of opinion, some asserting that Sherman would
have to move back to look after Hood, which
was Mr. Davis' idea, when he sent a soldier to
replace Joe Johnston, who would strike a
"manly blow," and who struck it at Franklin.

But old General Marcellus Brown here inter-
posed his opinion: "No, sir; no, sir; Sherman will come right on. He's got skilled engi-
neers and constructors who will build roads
faster than we can destroy them, and thousands
of our negroes will assist them; and who can
pilot them better than the black rascals, who
know every foot-path."

Col. Stout ventilates his patriotic estimation
of the "sacred soil of Carolina," and cannot
bring his mind to consider the possibility of its
profanation by the incendiary bummers of
Sherman's army.

Seated conspicuously in the midst of the group is an officer of the Confederate army, whose bright and unsoiled uniform, fair face and immaculate linen, are proofs positive against any charge of contact with war's rude buffetings; but bolstered by the kinsmanship of a power near the throne, usurps the place of men more deserving and better fitted for the duties incumbent upon him. Clearing his throat and waving out his dexter hand, he parades his views as follows: "At headquarters, I find a general disbelief of any foolhardy invasion of our country; we are entirely too far in the interior. I recently had the pleasure of a stroll with a visitor, or rather a refugee from Chattanooga, who gave Sherman but poor credit as a leader, and his army as merely a disorganized mob of bummers. He was highly pleased at the disposition of our means of defense, as well as of our forces; all of which I took the trouble to show and explain to him, and er—er— by-the-by" (with the most insinuating smile at having done so much for his friend) "he spoke of you most kindly, Captain Randolph, and said that you would be glad to hear from him, and made me the bearer of his greetings and best wishes for your welfare and success."

"I did not understand the name," remarks Randolph.

" Horton—Oh! yes, Van Horton. of Chattanooga," answers the Adjutant.

" Allow me then to say, Adjutant." answers
Randolph, whose flashing eyes and contracted
brows gave evidence of the awakening of the
lion in the man, " that your news is as disagreeable as it is unexpected. and that your *protege*
is an unrelenting enemy to our country; a
robber by taste and profession. false to you as
he was false to his own family. Your acts of
courtesy and hospitality were simply wasted upon
a spy."

Picture if you can, the surprise and mortifica-
tion of Adjutant Post. upon hearing the dreadful news. Embarrassed and confounded, the
holiday soldier leaves at the earliest opportunity.
and his absence enables the older heads to
ventilate their various disgusts of the recipient
of his knowledge of military facts.

To Marguerite it was nothing less than a
severe physical shock. " Van Horton here!"
the *bete noir* of the circle of friends in whose
safety and happiness her whole soul was concentrated. With a woman's watchful care of
the invalid one. Marguerite proposes to return
to the parlors, but her voice falls upon deaf ears,
and until her request is repeated. Randolph
arousing from his abstraction, apologizes for his
inattention and escorts her to her guests.

The handsome couple had hardly left the room before old General Marcellus Brown, with a thump upon the table to emphasize what he says: " That young man, Randolph, just suits me; says little, and that little he says well; sun-burned and scarred, he is the beau ideal of a soldier. Did you see him look at that pudding-head Post? He looked more like an awe-ning post when he left us."

"Oh, yes," says the host: "the men who have trotted with Jackson and Lee over the hills and vales of Virginia looking for fights, finding and winning them without counting the odds, are of just such stock. Now I, for one, am a believer in stock. I have fine stock at home, or did have until I gave them up to our government: and let me tell you, that careful breeding, training and handling are as essen-tially necessary to man as to the horse or other animal, and my opinion is that Post would have to be born again to be able to touch elbows with our invalid."

General Brown, laughing merrily, says: "Abe Lincoln has set an example as a high breeder. With a single dash of the pen he has created men, free men: voters without an idea of gov-ernment; jurymen without judgment; ignorant, superstitious, and but a generation removed from barbarism and cannibalism—all this with a dash

of the pen, which it took our fathers centuries
of patient struggle, study and privation to
secure and to be qualified to maintain. Be it
distinctly understood, gentlemen," he goes on,
" that I am not a lover of the institution of
slavery in the abstract, and recognize the love
of liberty which is implanted in the breast of
every living thing; yet this wholesale delivery,
this invitation to insurrection, murder and
arson, if not directly expressed, indirectly sug-
gested, burdens my mind with the belief that it
is the offspring of a cowardly brain, or a saving
expedient in a waning cause."

Our host, catching the infection, takes up the
subject as follows:

"Dropping the question of breeding, I have
read much and studied the everlasting negro, till
I am more convinced of his thorough unfitness
to occupy the position now designated for him
by the Lincoln proclamation; an act of usurpa-
tion and vindictiveness; the very quintescence
of malice, hatred and all uncharitableness. Go
back in history, yes, even to the days of Pharaoh,
and we find him then what he is now. For
four thousand years he has held undisputed
possession of a continent, yet he has never made
a law; the whole race is guiltless of the creation
of any work of art, a statue, a painting, or a
monument. With the wisdom, science and ex-

ample of every nation beaming upon them, it
has never penetrated their benighted haunts, nor
conquered their invincible ignorance. He is,
gentlemen, both morally and physically, a mys-
terious subject of God's unrelenting judgment,
incomprehensible as it is positive. In all past
time he has been a servant; a menial, and Abe
Lincoln and every other Lincoln on earth can
with all the appliances of law, philanthropy and
proclamation, only find him the same, either a
barber or in barbarism."

Having devoted this quantum of breath as a
kick and protest at old Abe's arbitrary move,
our host moves an adjournment to the society of
the ladies, and here they are met with news
which blanches the cheek of old and young
alike; it is the announcement that Savannah
had fallen, and that Sherman, with an immense
army, having plundered all the helpless old
women and children in a march through a thinly
settled country, with no opposing army, had
formed a junction with the Federal fleet off that
harbor, and had simply crowded out General
Hardee with his few Confederate regiments.

This wondrous achievement over hen-roosts
and helpless barnyards is yclept, after the maudlin sentimentality of a fawning press, "Sherman's March to the Sea," and which affords a
vent for patriotic Yankee schoolmarms by con-

tributing that operatic homily for school and church festivals entitled, "Marching Thro', Georgy."

The entertainment in honor of our hero, was a perfect success as a social gathering, Randolph meeting with many old friends among the ladies and among the cripples now occupying places requiring only easy service. But between the unpleasant introduction of Van Horton's name by Adjutant Post, and the news of the capture of Savannah, our hero retired, wondering "what would happen next?" but soon fell asleep to dream of "that fool, Post," verifying the truth of the adage, that we dream of that which is last upon the mind before sleeping.

Chapter XIII.

Right well did the gentleman from Chattanooga, the "so-called" refugee Van Horton, accomplish his mission. Relying upon his knowledge of the generous and unsuspicious hospitality of the Southern people, he found it no difficult matter to return directly to the advancing Yankee army, which he overtook just before its capture of Savannah.

His mission had been crowned with success, and his heart fairly leaped with joy at the knowledge of the solid reward which would inure to his credit for so meritorious a service in behalf of his commander.

Following him to his quarters, we find a merry crowd assembled under the shadow of a large "fly" which was raised in front of the tent, and served the purpose of mess-room, being supplied with camp-table and chairs.

The tent was pitched under a lovely old "live oak," whose garment of long, sweeping moss waved gently in the passing breeze.

Having just arrived after a long and dangerous trip, and an almost equally fatiguing search for his quarters, Van Horton, after dismounting, threw the rein in a careless manner to a negro boy, one of the many thousand following in the wake of Sherman's army, and bidding him to rub well, water and feed, dismissed all other considerations of horse or negro, and joins the mess, where he is received with many hand-shakes, many questions, with heavy slaps upon the shoulder, and last but not least, a pressing injunction to " drink, old fellow, it'll do you good."

" Say, fellows, what in the deuce could influ-ence an officer of the rank of colonel to take the chances of Van Horton's ride, unless there was a woman in the case?" Thus speaks one Lieu-tenant Peters.

" Oh, bosh! I can measure a man better than that," says Captain Burke. "for Van don't smile, and grin. and dawdle around. Look at him now. Don't you see confidence in his face? He is plump full of valuable information. Now catch on, and see if I am not right."

" Never mind a leetle about drawing close conclusions, shentlemens," says Captain Glass-sick, a jolly fat German with a jolly red nose; "youst eferybody fill up, undt let's drink a bumper to the arrival in der fold of our long lost sheeps," (and with military precision every glass is drained), and still standing. the rubi-cund German says: "Stand steady, shentlemans; undt come here, you black rascal, and make fill dose glasses;'' and continuing, he says: "Dot poy makes homesick mineself, for when he's aroundt I have dot odor of dose limberger mitoudt de beer, undt so I was all broke oudt. Now, shentlemans, I gifs a dost to dot fair lady I was entertaining yesterday and to the gallant officer she was looking for.''

With a clatter of glasses, a smacking of lips and many ejaculations, of "Oh!" "Oh!" "Oh!" the rotund Dutchman subsided, puffed up with the vanity of the possession of knowledge unknown to his comrades, and the anxiety to own the possession whereof would make him the center of a fire of inquiries, direct, plunging and cross, as to who she was, who she was looking for, etc.

While all was eagerness, their senses already inflamed by the liquor consumed, there was one who made no effort to find out by inquiry, for his mind was too intent upon the eager inward discussion as to "which one" it could be.

The phlegmatic Teuton smoked his pipe and smiled calmly at the wrangle, but never turned his gaze once upon Van Horton to signify that probably that it was he for whom the search was directed.

In an instant the babel of voices is hushed, for at a short distance from camp is discerned a lady rapidly approaching, sitting her horse with ease and grace, a jaunty little jockey-cap decorating her head, and long, dark green riding-skirt streaming in the wind, as her dashing sorrel sweeps along with light, springing strides.

Every man stops still; every one looks at one object. None know the coming equestrienne but one, and he, Van Horton, rising hurriedly, advances to meet her; courteously he salutes her, and leading her horse conducts the visitor to the "fly," and ceremoniously introduces Miss F—— as a vision of loyalty to the flag of the Union.

This is followed by more wine, and we are sorry to confess is participated in by Miss F——, who, possessed of every other attribute to make a fast woman, finds no trouble to add a decided taste for exhilerating drinks. In her most winning manner Miss F——, addressing Van Horton, asks: "Tell us what you have done, and what you know, for we are dying to hear."

"You will hear soon enough," answers Van Horton, "and headquarters shall be the first to hear; and as we have had our little recreation here, and you are well prepared, I will order my horse, ride over and report."

The Commander-in-Chief received Van Horton with expressions of marked gratification, and with closed doors his report was taken in detail. And as the weakness of resistance; the utter absence of men and means of defense; the unprotected homesteads, easy subjects for rapine and plunder, because occupied only by the helpless of both sexes, was shown in detail of the route northward via Columbia, Sherman's joy was boundless, and Van Horton was dismissed with words of gratitude and promises, which filled his breast with happy and buoyant hopes.

And from this moment begins the preparation for a movement which is to be quick and decisive. Within three days the whole army was under arms, and, crossing the Savannah river, moved northwardly in the direction of Columbia, the capital of the State of South Carolina.

CHAPTER XIV.

How wonderful are the powers of nature; in number without limit, in active operation in every phase of existence, animate and inanimate. One of the most intricate powers of nature is the mind of man. It is a store-house from which is drawn all that goes to make the wealth and happiness of the world, or that which brings ruin and despair to infinite numbers. While it makes the law, it breaks it and defies it. It defines the right, and is quick to aid the wrong. It is a worker of miracles. It has taught us to ride upon the winds; to whisper in the ear of our friends an hundred miles away; to write with the lightning's flash, and even to control the mind of others; but there is one power which, if ever given, is evidently lost—that of controlling ones own mind.

Thus it was with Randolph; sleeping or waking, his mind would dwell upon Van Horton's visit to Columbia. "What was he there for? Was he shadowing his movements, and was he, too, included in his scheme for vengeance, because of his kinship? or was he simply a spy, and Post the dupe of his machinations?"

Such was the state of his mind, that, coupled with his physical weakness, the hope of a speedy return to camp seemed to diminish, and his future to assume the form of a settled gloom.

This gloom had no silver lining, the smiles and happy presence of the lovely Marguerite, now dimly seen, seemed not able to dispel the leaden shadow.

It was a bright, sunny day, although it was crisp and cold out of doors; the family had partaken of a late dinner, and a bright, cheerful fire of wood burned upon the hearth of the parlor; and as Marguerite sat in a cosey arm-chair near the sofa, where Randolph reclined in a musing, pensive manner. so occupied was he in his own thoughts, which were none of the brightest, that the look of intense solicitude which was fixed upon him by Marguerite was entirely unnoticed, until Marguerite, remarking an ugly frown upon Randolph's face, accompanied by a motion of the lips and an upraised arm with a clenched hand, abruptly broke the the silence by asking: "Kind sir, are you quarreling with me, or am I to be the sole audience to your pantomimic program?"

Roused from his revery, Randolph answers as if awakened from a dream: "*Mille pardons, ma'mselle!* I was ruminating, reviewing my troubles. Between my impotence, loss of kin, friends, home, the curse of Van Horton, the vindictiveness of Miss F—, and last but not least, my separation from my command, I feel as if I was undergoing the agony of being drowned in a sea of troubles."

"Then my company goes for naught," says she.. "Who nursed you back to life, O, base ingrate?"

Upon his essaying to speak, smilingly, she shakes her finger at him and bids him to "repent and say something nice and pretty, something penetential, to show at least that the sense of gratitude is not entirely dead within you."

"My dear, I plead guilty to any charge of poverty of language to express, and my inability to repay you for your unselfish and untiring efforts in my behalf when so ill. May Heaven bless you, sweet one; but ungrateful—never! We have never had what others so often seem to crave, 'a lovers' quarrel,' and with God's help we never shall; but you must bear now with my depression, for I have for several days felt a sense of impending danger, an incubus of trouble, which I cannot account for, nor can I throw it aside."

"It is perfectly natural for morbid ideas to pervade the mind, when sickness seizes the body: or, perhaps, you may find some relief by piling the blame upon that poor, patient, and

D A—11

long-suffering member—the liver!" answers
Marguerite.

"No," answers Randolph. "my thoughts do
not seem the offshoot of anything morbid, nor
even the result of a torpid liver: it is, or will be,
all, I fear, but too real; and now please"——

There is a pause, for there came a loud ringing
of the front door-bell, which cut short any further
conversation, and in a few moments a servant
announced a lady, much to the surprise of both.

Marguerite saw before her timidly advancing,
a woman of lithesome figure, with hair, eyes
and complexion filling all the requisites of a
pronounced blonde; whose carriage betokened
a courage begotten of pride and right, but
whose sombre dress and wan and troubled expression appealed at once to the heart for aid,
comfort and protection.

Being seated, she handed Marguerite a note,
remarking as she did so that she was happy and
grateful to be the bearer of a missive from a dear
friend, Miss Sadie Carday, now visiting at
Washington, D. C., who so kindly volunteered
to introduce herself, who was en route south in
search of her husband, now Colonel Van Horton,
of the United States Army.

Here was a revelation, and with Randolph,
adding another stigma to the already stigmatized
Van Horton.

An expert mind reader would have found a task of extraordinary application, or perhaps would have been paralyzed at the expressions of amazement, sorrow, contempt and anger which pervaded the countenances of these three persons as they stood for a moment silently gazing at one another.

"Please excuse me," remarks Marguerite in her most courteous manner, "while I read Sadie's letter," which was as follows:

WASHINGTON, D. C., Jan. 15, 1865.

MY DEAR MARGUERITE—This will be handed to you by Mrs. Van Horton (really Mrs. A. Van Horton Darke), a native of England, in search of her husband, and who deserves all your sympathy as a true woman, and the innocent sufferer through the misdeeds of a heartless wretch.

She seeks not her husband to regain him, but for a purpose dearer to a mother's heart—to secure her child, taken from her in England, and who is reported to be with Van H——, or near him, under the charge of a Miss F—— or Mrs. Van Horton. Give her all the help and comfort you can. We caught up with Van Horton here, but when we thought we had him, he gave us the slip.

Nothing in this contraband, and a wounded and paroled prisoner kindly promised to see Mrs. Van H—— through safely.

Love and blessings.

Affectionately,

SADIE.

The elegance of manner, together with the friendless and pitiful condition of the poor stranger, was an impetus to each to suggest the best and surest method of finding the wretched abductor.

Randolph, however, with a soldier's suspicion, asks: "Why, Madam, did you not go direct by the Yankee route, as by following it you can more rapidly accomplish your purpose?"

With fiery energy, she answers: "I have no sympathy with the man or his cause; I desire only to *meet*, not to *follow* him."

So earnest were they, that it was late when Mrs. Van Horton (as we shall call her) took her leave, promising to return early the next morning and endeavor to secure passes from General Beauregard, now in command, and proceed to Savannah, via Augusta.

The next morning was ushered into life with a sun beaming with a beauteous luxuriousness almost preternatural, and as the rays came slanting in its first efforts to kiss the tops of the leafless trees, and warm with its sunny breath the frosts of night, every housetop in the City of Columbia seemed to reflect the glory of the god of day.

The beautiful city awoke to life, and, in the happy sunshine, the citizens engaged in their usual routine of business—thought not of murder, rapine and arson.

It was about 3 o'clock p. m., of the 15th of February, 1865, when a drooping, hard-ridden horse came slowly over the old, wooden bridge, spanning the Congaree river, bearing a cavalry-man, dusty and weary. A frank, handsome face, heavily moustached: broad shouldered, and with an old slouch hat cocked rakishly upon one side, he seemed the beau ideal of a man to trust upon a mission where danger required a quick eye, a strong arm, and plenty of nerve.

The rider knew his horse, for he was a part of him. The poor, dumb brute had served his master well; and, best of all, his master knew it, and loved him for it: and now, having passed the bridge and climbed the ascent to the railway, even passing the old freight-house, soon to be blown to atoms, our wearied horseman straightened up in his saddle, his animal felt the movement, and, quickly responding, hastened his pace, and soon he is at the door of the Nickerson, where General Beauregard had established his headquarters.

Very soon it transpires that this man has brought the message that Sherman, with his whole army, was in full march upon the helpless, undefended city.

The news was soon spread throughout the city, and many refugees, who had secured homes here, made haste again to decamp.

Many of all classes determined to brave it out. Their means were exhausted by the war, and they had no place to retreat, nor means of sustenance if they did.

Many prepared to leave, not caring to trust to the tender mercies of a foe who had plundered and burned a path through the unprotected homes and fields of helpless old men and innocent women.

On the arrival of Mrs. Van Horton, she found the whole house in confusion.

Randolph had gone to the front, with a few government clerks, some cavalry, and what was termed Home Guards (for the sake of euphony), but Marguerite was determined to stand her ground, and Mrs. Van H. was equally determined to cast her lot with her.

A widespread gloom settled down upon the whole city, and a hopeless resignation seemed to pervade the homes of all.

To those who had counted upon the magnanimity of the foe—"Sleep on; sleep for a little while!"—there will be a sad awakening, for there comes a hero (God save the mark) who has declared that "Columbia is as bad as Charleston," and that "Salt would hardly be necessary to sow upon its ruins."

Oh, brutal man! Is this the reward of one, trusted, honored, and placed in the highest position of a generous and unsuspecting people! *Nous verrons.*

CHAPTER XV.

ON the next afternoon, the 16th day of February, 1865, looking across the Congaree river to the hills about a mile beyond, there came borne upon the air the usual prelude of an advance, the "pop! pop! pop!" of the skirmish line. The evening was far advanced when the firing increased; and very soon could be seen a long, irregular line of ununiformed men swaying across an old field between two lines of trees. No flashing battle-flags to cheer the heart or to greet the eye; no veterans were there, only hastily improvised two-legged obstacles, which only meant *delay*.

With what thoughts did each one regard this panorama, as Marguerite and her guest watched the exciting but hopeless scene?

Soon darkness settled over the scene, and with burning stores and cotton, the movement of troops, principally cavalry, the sad hearts of the populace wore out a sleepless night, but scarcely realized a foretaste of the dreadful experience in store for them.

The next day, February 17th, the Federal troops threw their shells into the city, and without opposition, marched in and took possession, Sherman marking his supercillious entry by his vulgar discourtesy to the Mayor, who met him upon entering.

The terrible day wore away into the darkness of the night. The helpless, young and old, now worn with watching and dreading the vengeance of the oppressor, were suddenly aroused to anxious wakefulness by the cry of "fire! fire!"

Soon the city was illumined by the flames arising simultaneously from different points of the compass. The residents then saw and felt their doom.

The flames spread rapidly from house to house; drunken soldiers looted *ad libitum*. Men, women and children rushed hither and thither, frantic with fear; or, over-eager to save their property, lost all by attempting to appease the rapacity of their despoilers by offering a part. Some to seek safety from personal harm, lifted the sick upon cots and litters to the middle of the street, where the full view of the terrible scene made the hope of safety mockery by adding horror to danger.

The Carnival of Arson and Deviltry went on in every form of crime known to rapine, robbery, lust and vengeance.

Marguerite and her guest were so paralyzed with fear that neither could realize the extent of the conflagration, as the place was filled with soldiers in every phase of temper and intoxication, either burning or stealing.

The fire went on in its consuming course, nearly destroying the beautiful city by sweeping away everything from the State House on the south to the distance of about one mile northwardly; and what had once been thickly studded with handsome and substantial brick buildings, occupied as stores, offices, hotels, etc., was one solid ruin: and on each side a distance of from one to three blocks thoroughly Shermanized.

Could Sherman have ever seen the order of the Christian soldier, which we so proudly here append?

"HEADQUARTERS, ARMY NORTHERN VIRGINIA,

"CHAMBERSBURG, PA., June 27, 1863.

"It must be remembered that we make war only upon armed men, and that we cannot take vengeance for the wrongs our people have suffered without lowering ourselves in the eyes of all whose abhorrence has been excited by the attrocities of our enemy, without offending against Him to whom vengeance belongeth; without whose favor and support our efforts must all prove in vain. The Commanding General, therefore, earnestly exhorts the troops to abstain, with most scrupulous care, from unnecessary or wanton injury to private property, etc.

"R. E. LEE, *General.*"

The night wore slowly away, the breeze stirring the flickering embers, and the smoke still hovering over the crumbling ruins. Worn out with the bacchanalian orgies of the night, and weary and weighted with plunder, the soldiers slept until the day again broke over a city conquered, plundered, and in ashes.

Having satisfied his burning desire to take the city, Sherman had also satisfied his desire to burn it, and now he began his march to leave the ashes of the mighty camp-fire of his vengeance.

So horror-struck with the reckless destruction of private property, and a witness of the crimes and excesses committed by the bummer troops, too horrible to relate, Mrs. Van Horton was loath to trust her presence to the tender mercies of the marching army.

Believing that Randolph's physical condition would soon force him back, or that he would soon return to relieve their necessities, as they were despoiled of the very necessities of life and would starve without help, Marguerite advised a patient wait for his arrival.

On the day of Sherman's entry into the city, Randolph joined a body of cavalry under General H——, at Littleton, seven miles north of Columbia, as a volunteer, and proceeded with them to Newberry, to assist in driving off detached bands of Yankee raiders.

Hearing early of the destruction of Columbia,

he secured supplies immediately, and took the main road going down the valley of the Saluda river, his wagon heavily laden with provisions for the now destitute citizens.

From Newberry to Columbia is about forty miles, and along the entire route Randolph saw naught but ashes and a widespread desolation. Where but a few days before stood the happy homes of helpless youth and defenceless age, there stood only the bare chimneys, the silent, solemn monuments marking the path of plunder, arson, rape and wanton destruction.

The silent ruin nevertheless spoke to the heart, and Randolph was oppressed beyond measure. He had participated in all the campaigns in Virginia, Maryland and Pennsylvania where soldier met soldier armed and equipped for battle; where fields were covered with the dead and dying, victims of war's insatiate thirst for blood; yet never before had such a cruel and relentless exhibition of uncivilized and barbarous warfare, and desecration of the property and sacred rights of non-combatants met his gaze before.

Time, time cures many a rugged wound; and it is well said that he who forgives not, breaks down the bridge over which he must cross: but in future time, when the truth of history will be known, will it not be a blight upon a hero's (?) escutcheon, to stand convicted as the author and

abettor of such infamy? And in an age like
this, the age of steam and electricity, the *Nine-
teenth Century*, the apotheosis of civilization!

Crossing the river to the Columbia side, Randolph wended his way through the burnt district
to the home of Marguerite, and to his mortifica-
tion found her absent, but was solaced by the
joy of her father, who was rapturous in his praise
of the timely arrival, claiming that he had re-
versed the parable of the Prodigal Son.

No time was to be lost; people were in want
of the necessaries of life, and old Captain Darlington claimed that he had in no wise left his
code of Old Virginia hospitality behind him.

Not forgetting the venerable Doctor who had
attended him when so near death's door, Randolph desired to supply him first. Upon arriving at his gate he went no further, for there was
not a vestige of his pretty home.

The Doctor was a man of noble physique,
noble in character and striking in appearance—
a man who stood first in his profession in the
city and the State—and his home was the fruits
of a lifetime of laborious service.

Decorating the walls of his mansion were the
pictured forms and faces of those who had fig-
ured in the history of their country's glory; of
a son who was slain in the celebrated charge of
the Carolina troops in the bloody battle of

RANDOLPH MEETS THE DOCTOR.
A SHERMAN MONUMENT.

Buena Vista in Mexico, and whose name is emblazoned upon the pedestal of the bronze Palmetto monument in the Capitol grounds of Columbia.

While Randolph contemplated the sad scene, the old Doctor came along, simply from force of habit, and espied his patient, and with the same calm demeanor which always characterized him expressed his happiness in beholding his improved condition. Not one word of complaint passed the old man's lips, though homeless and suffering from hunger.

Randolph, clasping his hand, said: "Doctor, you have my heartfelt sympathy, and I have come as your temporary commissary and desire to issue rations."

"Thanks, Captain; many thanks. Your arrival is very opportune; my children and orphan grandchildren are sorely in need. You see our shelter is gone and our rations went at the same time."

"Tell me, Doctor, how they came to burn your place—you, a much-needed man among the sick, and a non-combatant?"

"Why they destroyed my premises, I cannot tell; how they did, I can. I was called away in the very height of the conflagration to attend a lady patient. I left my children and grandchildren with my housekeeper, (my wife being dead). I was absent about an hour, when upon my return, I found my children shivering with cold and fear upon the front porch, and a number of Federal soldiers moving up and down the stairs, sacking the house. As I stepped upon the porch a soldier went to the parlor door and shook it (it being locked). He asked, 'What's in here?' I, referring to my portraits, answered, ' None but the dead.' They then came out upon the porch, threw inflammable liquid upon the siding and floor, struck matches and fired my home. I turned to my children and said, 'Come.' We left and saved nothing, not one single item.''* And as they turned their backs upon the blackened ruins, they directed their steps to the home of Marguerite.

To tell the truth, Randolph was thinking of his darling little girl, but the good Doctor, taking another view of his silence and abstraction, proceeded to say: "I will not revive sad memories in my own breast, nor tire you with the harrowing details of the night of the 17th of February, 1865; they are known to our Father in Heaven who hath said, 'vengeance is mine, I will repay.' My dear Captain, crimes were committed too horrible to relate—excesses marked by the cruel invention and barbarous vulgarity of untamed savages.''

*True, verbatim.

With this, the subject is dropped; for there upon the veranda, in all the glory of her Confederate " Bee Store" calico, stood Marguerite, whose smiling face was as radiant with happiness as a heart filled with love, satisfied and glorified, could make it, awaiting the return of her patient lover, now impatiently.

Catching the contagion. Randolph, feeling quite as happy, and perhaps more so, cries out, "Is it I or the rations?"

"The rations, of course, you darling old fellow," answers Marguerite. "You have come in the nick of time. Although they did not burn our home, they took all that we had, and turned up the whole yard with their bayonets, seeking for buried treasure. Bless your soul," laughingly, she says, "but are they not experts? Not quite smart enough to get our little engagement ring, with my few remaining articles of jewelry; for my maid, Julia, lifted a fence-post in the stableyard, and put back the post upon my fortune, and lo! they are here, safe."

And thus the afternoon passes away. The kind, old Doctor had left several hours before; tea had been served, and, as it was growing late, the family were preparing to retire, when a messenger brought to Randolph a note from the surgeon in charge of the hospital, asking his

immediate attendance at the special request of
Mrs. Van Horton.

Donning his military overcoat, and looking
well to his "navy six," he soon found himself
at the office of the hospital, where an attendant
was awaiting to conduct him to the ward in
which the surgeon was engaged. .

Proceeding thither, he was ushered into a
large, airy room, containing a single cot, upon
which a man was lying. Bending over him
stood the surgeon, while Mrs. Van Horton stood
near, holding a basin of water. To an old soldier, it was evident they were dressing the
wounds of some unfortunate.

All was still—no word was spoken—and the
little clock upon the mantel merrily clicked
away the minutes of time, careless of their value
to the patient, whether living or dying.

With a look of thanks from the woman, and
a nod of recognition from the doctor, Randolph
entered with noiseless steps, and looked down
upon the mangled form of Colonel Van Horton!

When Columbia had fallen into the hands of
the invaders, Sherman ordered the shot and
shell stored in the magazine of the State arsenal
on the hill, near the reservoir of the city, to be
loaded upon wagons and to be thrown into the
river, by a detail of forty or fifty men.

Van Horton was superintending the casting

of the shell into the Congaree river, when, by some unaccountable mishap, an explosion occurred, killing every man of the detail and fatally wounding the officer (Van H.) in charge—literally annihilating soldiers, mules and wagons.*

Having accounted for Van Horton's condition, we will proceed with our story.

The continued efforts of the surgeon, ably assisted by the discarded wife, soon told upon the suffering man, for, after a few moments, he gradually aroused from his lethargy, coolly surveyed his surroundings, and recognizing and fixing his gaze upon the woman whom he had so grievously wronged, faintly asked, "Is it possible?"

Being moved by a sense of pity, the poor woman approached the sufferer with tearful eyes and outstretched arms, with an effort, once more to press her head upon the bosom of him who had pledged to love, honor and protect her, when the door was suddenly opened from without, and. like an apparition, a tall, handsome blonde. elegantly attired, and leading a handsome boy of six or seven years, glided into the room with almost abrupt haste. and with the manner and assurance of one both privilged and expected.

Not understanding anything of the history of the parties here strangely met, the doctor, who

---

*True.   D A—12

had been closely watching his patient, who desired to meet with Randolph before bidding farewell to earth, turned to Randolph, and was almost startled by the expression of his face; his hands were clenched, his eyes blazing with wrath. What could have aroused such an exhibition of anger and hate by the mere appearance of a woman in the act of rendering a friendly service to a suffering soldier? This was the question that flashed through the doctor's mind.

Not long did he have to wait to have his question solved. Thinking Randolph to be in Virginia with his command, Miss F——, in her haste scarcely noticed the presence of any one except that of Van Horton and the surgeon attending.

Closing his eyes upon her entrance, Van Horton's quietude, with that of every one else, made the stillness of the room almost death-like, until Mrs. Van Horton, who had stood spell-bound upon the intruder's entrance, and had fixed a long, loving look upon the child introduced, gave a cry of joyful recognition, which startled her hearers, and was strangely echoed through the dimly lighted halls.

The scene which followed would require the genius of an Edgar Allen Poe to present, for what followed was beauty, deceit and sin entrapped, then expelled; hope, love and honor

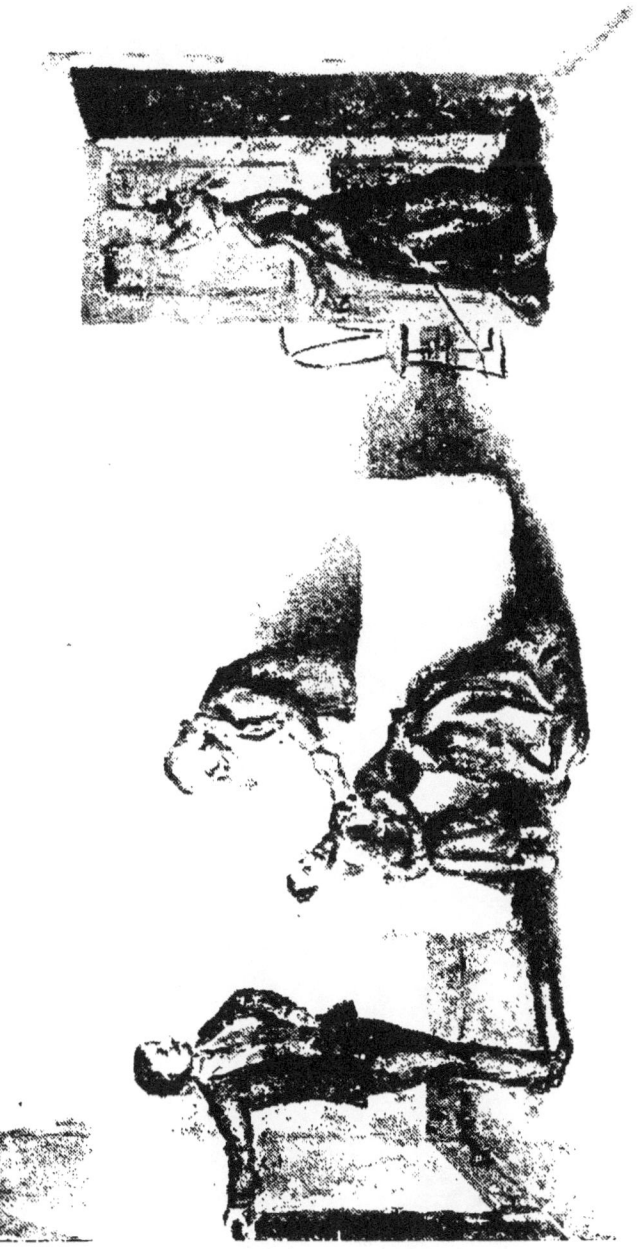

rewarded, and the heart made glad; and to the now poor, helpless sufferer the knowledge of God's good pledge "Vengeance is mine. I will repay."

The piercing cry had scarcely died away. when Van Horton, stretching forth his right arm. the only uninjured limb, and raising his head, pointed to the child now in its mother's arms, and said: "'Tis hers—1—I have failed."

To Randolph—"You have her (pointing to Miss F——) to thank for all my work of vicious hate. I know that I have to die, and I want your forgiveness."

And to his wife, very feebly: "Can you forgive me, Grace?"

The poor, heart-broken woman, wife-like, forestalling his thoughts. even his desires. held the child's quivering lips to his parting kiss, and clasping the weary head to her bosom, saw and felt the breath going by gasps from the poor, shattered body, while Randolph held his hand and assured him that he was forgiven, as he hoped to be forgiven.

It was but a few moments when all was over, and the little one fatherless.

During the death scene, Miss F—— had weighed well that the meeting with Randolph was not a matter of trifling interest, both on account of her acts of a personal character.

and her association as a unit in the invading
army.

With that cat-like quietness and alertness
which characterized her movements, she disappeared unseen, nor was her departure noted or
cared for; like a cigar stump it was smoked out,
and the remains went to the gutter; but in long
years after, the lightning of her unscrupulous
wrath flashed through sombre clouds of news-
paper slings.

In a few days Van Horton slept with the sod
above him, which he had so lately trod as con-
queror, his wife and little one awaiting a steamer
at Charleston.

When Colonel Van Horton was picked up
after the explosion, with shattered limbs and
mortal wounds, the news traveled like a flash to
his camp quarters, where Miss F—— and his
child were cosily enjoying a siesta in the deserted
premises of a prominent refugee.

Leaving the child, she hurried to the scene of
devastation, to find that the Colonel had been
conveyed to the nearest hospital, which was in
use by the Confederates. Hastening thither,
she was informed that he was then unconscious,
and that his wounds were mortal. Tired and
depressed, she sat down by his cot to await the
return of consciousness.

Long did the moments seem, but at last there

came a long-drawn sigh, a moan of pain, as
nature came back to assert its claims and to
resent its abuse, and with lips contracted with
pain, received the kiss of his visitor.

Knowing his desperate condition, he said in a
mandatory tone:

" Go, bring my boy, that I may see him once
more before I die," and acting promptly the
fear inspired by his words and his condition oper-
ating as an impetus to her movements, she hastened away and soon accomplished her errand,
with the result already described. Ignorant of
the happenings while upon her errand, Miss
F——, with her proverbial recklessness, rushed
into the presence of those who loathed her very
name.

And now we relegate her to her bummer associates, and waive her adieu forever, to resume
the thread of our story.

Randolph and Marguerite made frequent
tours about the city, and contributed in no
small manner toward the alleviation, if not the
relieving of the distress of many families.

Deep and bitter was the denunciation of Sherman for his inhuman barbarity in the unnecessary destruction of one of the fairest cities of
ths South.

And now, thirty years after, let us pause for
a few moments to consider the facts in the noble

effort to obtain the *truth* of *history*, asserting only what we know, and quoting from Sherman himself, who tells of his cruel and unwarrantable crime of looting and burning Columbia.

In the Memoirs of W. T. Sherman, written by himself, page 287, Vol. II., occurs these words: " In my official report of this conflagration, I distinctly charged it to General Wade Hampton, and confess I did so *pointedly to shake the faith of his people in him;* for he was in my opinion a braggart, and professed to be the champion of South Carolina."

Was there ever a more puerile sentence written than this—a spiteful, jealous, emanation of a mimic historian?

If there was ever one name the least applicable in the language of every people upon God's earth, the name of braggart connected with that of Hampton is the one. It may be handed down only in Sherman's book, but an incendiary, indicted by a civilized world, and proven by the words of his own mouth, can never besmirch the character of so gallant a gentleman.

Did Hampton's cotton and torch reach forty miles, cross the Congaree and Saluda rivers, rest for hours from its labor of love and affection to his old friends, neighbors and kinsmen, and then burn Columbia and despoil the home of his wife and children?

Sherman burned Columbia—contemplated it, and carried out his contemplation to the letter, his denial to the contrary notwithstanding, and his Memoirs prove the truth of the assertion.

See page 152, Volume II, to show his animus, his incendiary propensity: "Until we repopulate Georgia it is useless to occupy it, but by the utter destruction of its roads, *houses*" (not its armies), etc., * * * "we can make this march and make Georgia howl."

Again, page 159, Volume II, "I sally forth to ruin Georgia." Not one word of fighting—only of the looting and barbarous destruction of the homes of helpless non-combatants—old men, women and children.

On entering South Carolina, in Sherman's general order No. 120, page 175, Volume II, this appears: "Section 5. To corps commanders alone is entrusted the power to destroy houses."

Halleck wrote from the City of Washington, December 18, 1864 (see page 228, Volume II): "Should you capture Charleston, I hope that by *some accident* the place may be destroyed, and if a little salt should be sown upon its site," etc.

To Halleck, in answer, Sherman writes (see *idem*): "I will bear in mind your *hint* as to Charleston, and do not think that salt will be necessary. When I move, the Fifteenth Corps will be on the right of the right wing, and their position will naturally bring them into Charleston first, and if you have watched the history of that corps, you will have remarked that they generally do their work pretty well. The truth is, the whole army is burning with an insatiable desire to wreak vengeance on South Carolina. I almost tremble at her fate. but feel that she deserves *all that seems in store for her. I look upon Columbia as quite as bad as Charleston.*"

And true to his promise to Halleck, the Fifteenth Corps was the first to enter Columbia. "which was quite as bad as Charleston;" the "same accident" did occur. and the place was laid in ashes.

How, in the face of all this. and thousands of eye-witnesses. could Sherman have the unblushing affrontery "to charge it to General Wade Hampton?"

To falsify his denial by an open and honest confession, which. perhaps, he conceived. according to the teachings of an old adage, would work some benefit for his soul, was a crowning act of his literary digest. and occurs on page 288. Volume II, of his Memoirs: "Having utterly ruined Columbia, the right wing began its march northward."

After maturing a march. poetically to the sea (really against old men, women and children, all helpless and defenseless), by a general order systematically arranging details for marauding and plunder, in the bitterness of his venom he ruthlessly loots and burns, and, appalled at the enormity of his crime, most lamely attempts to shift the burden upon the shoulders of an honorable soldier.

Oh, no! General Sherman. Hampton was no descendant of the *burning* race; nor was his sword ever drawn upon old men, women and children, but under his superior officer, the *Great Lee*, he was expressly forbidden such, and, by general order, reminded that "Vengeance was only the prerogative of his Maker."

Apropos just here, a little incident we beg to mention—a jewel worth unveiling.

When Barksdale's sharpshooters, before Fredericksburg, destroyed the pontooniers, and impeded the construction of the pontoon bridge, it so provoked the general of side-whiskers fame— *the Burnside*—that forgetting the men with arms in their hands, he turned one hundred and forty-seven pieces of artillery upon the devoted city, driving hundreds of women and children from their homes, to wander over the frozen highway, thinly clad, and knowing no place of refuge, their miserable path lighted up by the lurid glare of their own homes and the bursting shells of one hundred and forty-seven guns.

General Lee grimly watched the painful spectacle from a redoubt, silently noting the wanton destruction; then gravely turning to those near him, remarked: " These people delight to destroy the weak and those who can make no defense; *it just suits them.*"

Let this be Sherman's epitaph.

We honor men like Grant; cool in the midst of all troubles, honorable and just in his dealings, a hero who faced death on a hundred battlefields, and twice on his bed of sickness; a soldier who sought his armed enemy and gave him battle—all honor to the noble warrior! The prayers of every good soldier goes up to the great, White Throne for such as him. But Sherman!—and his march to the sea—from all such, " Good Lord deliver us," is a fixture in our Litany.

With an armed force of one hundred and twelve thousand men; more than Hood, Beauregard, Hardee, Johnston and Lee combined, with no army to oppose; only the frightened faces of old men, women and children, with a *finale* of a *grand negro round-up*—this, O, shades of Cæsar! is the theme of pæans of " Sherman's March to the Sea!"

Chapter XVII.

Six months have elapsed since the events last related occurred. War-clouds have rolled by, and the sun of peace is shining down upon a country whose people are once more engaged in the pursuits of industry and commerce.

Now and then a crutch or an empty sleeve, brings back the remembrance of the din and carnage of battle, but the bummers of the camps are loath to quit their occupation, and have now become the bummers of politics.

Under the name of reconstruction, the South is undergoing a moral trial from which she emerged with shorn locks but with spirits renewed, with rejuvenated vigor, with a healthy, chastened energy.

And now, as the leaves are beginning to be tinged by the chilling touch of frost, when the fall roses are unfolding their fresh, sweet buds to greet the sunbeams and cheer the heart and eye of man; when the robins come trooping with their happy chirps overhead, filling the tree-tops with their welcome voices; just in this time and season we find the same two persons in the same garden, at the same spot, as when long months ago we found them, after their eventful boat ride.

Then, it was on the eve of a departure upon an errand of grim-visaged war: but now it is upon the eve of quite a different journey.

A journey of life—for now, after so many years of faithful waiting. Marguerite and Randolph are to be united in the holy bonds of wedlock.

And here, among so many kindred and friends, there were but few houses where the one important subject was not discussed in every phase conceivable and inconceivable, from cellar to garret, and from kitchen to stable.

Old Captain Darlington and his good Virginia wife were proud of their children and of him to be numbered among them, and were determined that the temporary dwelling of balloon construction, (his beautiful home having been burned by Hunter's forces in his raid) should be no drawback upon the celebration of these nuptials, which should partake of all the forms and festivities of an old-fashioned Virginia wedding.

The days have gone by, and old Time has sprinkled our heads with frosty marks of his seasons passed, but never will he be able, with all his chilly breath, to cool or dim the remembrance of that happy event.

The sun had set in a clear, blue sky, and the

quivering leaves of fall barely felt the passing breeze; the stars looked down, twinkling, from their dark, blue canopy, and all was peace— peace, sweet peace.

All hearts thronging there were happy, and nature inanimate seemed in glorious unison with nature animate. The very barking of the dogs, scurrying through the lane, seemed happy and cheerful.

Up among the grove of trees, there streamed a flood of light through every window. Many of the old servants, surfeited with a few months of philanthropic Yankee servitude, were back at home, and by the antics of the picaninnies, and the "hi-hi's" and "yah! yah's!" of their elders, accompanied by the arrival of buggies, carriages, and every other vehicle owned or ob- tainable, created a pandemonium of joyous con- fusion.

Kindred met kindred, after years of absence in camp or prison. Old friends came from the valleys of the James, the Shenandoah and the Roanoke.

Beautiful women, whose dear hands had so lately smoothed the brows of dying soldiers, or cheered their lovers in their devotion to their country, were there.

Give me for courage, hospitality and the true temper of the patriotic Roman matron, the

woman of blessed Old Virginia! Glorious old
Mother, the synonym of heroine!

The clock had just chimed the hour of ten,
when the minister of God, robed in the surplice
of his holy office, made his appearance in their
midst, prepared to perform the functions of his
calling.

A grim smile wreathed the face of many an
old soldier. He pictured in his mind the slight
contrast of another occasion, wherein our same
surpliced minister, officiating in another capac-
ity, upon the historic field of Manassas, turned
loose his artillery with the benediction, ''and
may the Lord have mercy upon their souls!''

There was a stillness of expectant surprise,
when the curtains were drawn aside, nor were
their expectations disappointed, for as Marguerite stood leaning upon the arm of the gallant
Randolph, never was beauty more radiantly
pictured.

Decked with the simplicity of a village maiden,
no queen, with all the robes of state and jewels
of a nation's vaults, could excel the wealth of
beauty, of form and of feature, and of the luxu-
rious gifts of nature's own hands; as the loving
pair stood and pledged their troth, and received
the benediction of the brave old minister of
God.

It is years since that event, and now far

away west of the Mississippi river, Randolph watches the playful antics of a smaller Sadie, and a Lawrence, too, and often reminds Marguerite that when he shook the dust of the Institute from his feet he dreamed but little of finding his fair bride among the ashes of Columbia, and his nuptials over the ashes of her father's homestead.

FINIS.

www.ingramcontent.com/pod-product-compliance
Lightning Source LLC
Chambersburg PA
CBHW020618030726
47497CB00007B/2300